Edward Herbert Maxwell

With the Connaught Rangers in Quarters, Camp, and on Leave

Edward Herbert Maxwell

With the Connaught Rangers in Quarters, Camp, and on Leave

ISBN/EAN: 9783337424893

Printed in Europe, USA, Canada, Australia, Japan

Cover: Foto ©Andreas Hilbeck / pixelio.de

More available books at **www.hansebooks.com**

WITH

THE CONNAUGHT RANGERS

IN

QUARTERS, CAMP, AND ON LEAVE.

BY

GENERAL E. H. MAXWELL, C.B.,

AUTHOR OF "GRIFFIN AHOY!"

LONDON:

HURST AND BLACKETT, PUBLISHERS,

13, GREAT MARLBOROUGH STREET.

1883.

CONTENTS.

CHAPTER I.

THE CONNAUGHT RANGERS.

CHAPTER II.

IN THE WEST INDIES.

CHAPTER III.

ENGLAND AND THE CONTINENT.

CHAPTER IV.

IN TURKEY AND THE CRIMEA.

CHAPTER V.

THE PUNJAUB.

CHAPTER VI.

DELHI.

CHAPTER VII.

THE AMEER OF CABUL.

CHAPTER VIII.

CASHMERE.

CHAPTER IX.

THE VALE OF CASHMERE.

CHAPTER X.

THE MAHARAJAH.

CHAPTER XI.

VALLEY OF THE SCIND.

CHAPTER XII.

THE RESIDENT OF CASHMERE.

CHAPTER XIII.

TRAVELLING IN CASHMERE.

CHAPTER XIV.

FAREWELL TO CASHMERE.

CHAPTER XV.

THE HIMALAYAS.

CHAPTER XVI.

OUR FINAL JOURNEY.

CHAPTER I.

THE CONNAUGHT RANGERS.

CHAPTER I.

IN the year 1839 I entered the Army as ensign
in the 88th Regiment Connaught Rangers,
which was then quartered in Dublin; and a
merry life it was. What with drill and parties,
hunting and field-days, the officers of the old
regiment were always occupied. There were
several packs of hounds within easy distance of
Richmond Barracks; but the Ward Union was
the one most patronised by my brothers-in-arms.
The manœuvres in the Phœnix Park were not
much varied. I remember one day, when, my
captain being absent, I was in command of the
company in which I was ensign. The old colour-
sergeant took the greatest care of me. We
advanced in line, and so sure was the non-commissioned officer of what the manœuvre would
be that he whispered to me: 'When ye get to
that black thing on the ground, ye must give

the words, "Form fours to the right; right wheel;"' which, I think, was the form in those days. The black thing was a crow, which flew away before we got up to it. But, by my friend the colour-sergeant's help, I gave the proper word, and we retired in time to let the cavalry through. Week after week passed, and the same manœuvres were executed.

Old Toby White was town-major then, and his portrait, often repeated, appeared on the walls of the Castle Guard. I always tried to be sub. on the Castle Guard, for it was a pleasant lounge during the day, and in the evening a good dinner was served free of expense, while at night a supper of grilled bones, etc., was always ready for those who had been at the theatre, and who looked in on their way home.

Everything is changed in Ireland now-a-days. The spirit of fun seems to have vanished, and a sombre gloom appears to overshadow every-thing. There was always a comical side to all the proceedings of our Irish friends, even when the affair was serious, or assumed an air of importance.

I remember going to Donnybrook fair—now

a thing of the past—with two brother officers, Bayley and Dawson. When we arrived all was quite decorous. We observed many tents, in which the country people were apparently enjoying themselves peaceably, but, unfortunately, an urchin—a Dublin street Arab—came up to us, and said, 'Give me half-a-crown, captin, and I'll show ye the finest sport ye ever saw.' So we tossed him the money, and off he went. He crept up near a tent, where we saw him 'feeling for a head,' and, having found one 'convanient' belonging to some man inside, perhaps asleep, he took the stick in his hand, and hit the head as hard as he could. The effect was wonderful. All started up with such vehemence that the tent came down at once, and everyone began to fight with his neighbour. The clatter of sticks was incessant, and the uproar soon extended to the whole fair. Then the peelers rushed in, and were swayed from one side to the other by the contending parties. We left the scene of battle while the strife was still raging,—many a cracked crown being the consequence of that miserable half-crown.

After being quartered for some time in Dublin, we were ordered to Cork, there to await embarkation to Malta. In the year 1840, affairs in Syria looked very warlike, and we fully expected to be ordered on to the seat of war, but the bombardment of St. Jean D'Acre by our Fleet, under Sir R. Stopford, together with the other successful operations, put off for some years a great war.

The 42nd Royal Highlanders were quartered at Cork when we were there, and a great friendship existed between the two regiments. The consumption of whiskey—to cement this friendly feeling—among the men of the two corps was enormous. Sometimes a Highlander and a Connaught Ranger might be seen climbing the steep hill on whose summit the infantry barracks are situated; both having proved the genuineness of their friendship by deep potations, and both in their way showing various indications of their respective nationalities. Sandy appeared quiet, grave, and canny, while Paddy was excited and noisy; waving a stick in the air, and challenging everyone to 'tread on the tail of his coat.'

When they arrived at the barrack-gate, the Scotchman pulled himself together, and, solemnly fixing his eyes on a distant point, marched steadily past the sentry to his barrack-room, while the Irishman, howling defiance to all about him, staggered right into the middle of the guard and was lodged most probably in a cell for the night.

At length the transport *Conway* was reported to be ready to receive the head-quarters of the Connaught Rangers, and we went on board. Very different from what they are now were the vessels employed for the conveyance of troops; the comfort and luxury of floating palaces like the *Crocodile* and the *Jumna* were then unknown, and a ship that was considered almost unsafe to convey merchandise was regarded as quite good enough to carry one of Her Majesty's regiments.

A curious scene the deck of our old East Indiaman presented when we got on board. Confusion seemed the order of the day; geese, ducks, and fowls filling the air with their peculiar cries. It was difficult to get along the decks, so crowded were they with friends of the soldiers, consisting of weeping women and disconsolate children.

Somehow or other every stranger was cleared

out in the course of time, and we put to sea. We had a very rough time of it in the Bay of Biscay, for it blew a fierce gale from the S.W., and not only could we make no way against the storm, but we were driven quite out of our course. These discomforts were not much thought of by my young brothers-in-arms, but must have been trying to the older officers on board. One veteran attached to our regiment passed a fearful time. He had never been to sea before, having served always in a cavalry corps, and the extent of his voyages had been from England to Ireland and back again; he was an old man now, and he and his wife had a very miserable appearance. Whenever he came into the cabin he looked the picture of woe, but I fear he got no sympathy from us youngsters. Once when the storm was at its worst, and the waves broke clean over the ship, the green water washing in at the cuddy door, 'Oh!' exclaimed the poor old man, 'why do we not go into a harbour? Can we not get a steamer to tow us in?' This proved an unfortunate remark to make in the presence of a lot of careless young jokers.

'A first-rate idea,' said one of them. 'Let

us get up a subscription for a steamer to pull us out of this tre-men-duous sea.' No sooner said than done. We got a sheet of paper and wrote the following heading: 'It is proposed to get a steamer to tow us out of the Bay of Biscay. Officers wishing to subscribe towards a fund to pay the expense of the said steamer are requested to sign their names.' We all wrote down the amount we were willing to give, some putting down five pounds, others two pounds; but the poor old man, who was considered by us to be rather fond of his money, surprised us all by putting down his name for twenty pounds. The paper was stuck up in the cabin, but the old captain of the transport baffled our project, and let the cat out of the bag by asking the ancient warrior, 'How the dickens are ye to get at the steamer?' I do not think we were ever forgiven for our rather cruel joke.

On our arrival at Malta we were hospitably entertained by the regiments quartered there. The season was a very gay one, as our magnificent sailing fleet almost filled the many harbours, and dinners and balls, regattas and races, became the order of the day. The race-course was a very primitive affair, being a hard road called Pieta; but great was the excitement of these sporting events when the 'Wandering Boy,' belonging to Captain Horsford of the Rifle Brigade, won the Ladies' Whip, and Major Shirley's (88th regiment) 'Monops' came in first for some other favourite stakes.

I shall pass over the three years I belonged to the Malta garrison, during which time I went a cruise to Candia and Greece. The late Admiral of the Fleet, Sir Houston Stewart, was then captain of the *Benbow*, in which I went as guest of the present Admiral Sir John Hay, then a mate. A more delightful time no man ever had, for the *Benbow* was celebrated for its hospitality, and all the officers were kindness itself. To recall these pleasant hours is the most agreeable exercise of an old soldier's memory, but the old ship is now a hulk. Her captain rests in his honoured grave, and the jolly young *Benbows* of that merry time have become admirals and captains, and are all scattered to the four winds. I had often intended visiting Naples and Rome, but somehow the journey never came off, the remarks made by an old colonel having probably had some effect in preventing me from undertaking the journey. When he was asked if he enjoyed his visit to Rome, he always got very angry, an anger which increased to fury if one mentioned any of the ruins. 'Ah, bah!' he would exclaim, 'the Colay-sayem, is it? —the greatest absurdity that ever stepped—just a parcel of ould stones!'

In 1843 I left Malta, and, after a few months' leave, I was ordered to join the dépôt of the 88th, quartered at Paisley. The dépôt of a regiment in those days was a miniature battalion, consisting of four companies, under command of a major. We were particularly fortunate in our commanding officer, who always was kind and considerate to everyone. We also had a good band—a privilege which a dépôt was allowed to enjoy at that time.

Very soon after joining at Paisley, I was sent on detachment to Dumbarton Castle. My party consisted of a sergeant, a corporal, and twenty men. When at Paisley, I was provided with a servant—a stately old soldier named Thomas Pillsworth, but better known afterwards as 'Illustrious Tom.' His wife, one of the fattest women I ever saw, became my housekeeper at Dumbarton. The rock of Dumbarton is a lonely spot, and to a young fellow of twenty-one was regular banishment. For a day or two I sat on the top of the rock and moaned over my sad fate, but very soon all became changed, for I was most kindly received by the families in the county, and I look back to the period of my being quartered in Dumbarton Castle as a most agreeable reminiscence. When I was there, I was known as ' the governor of the castle.' My command consisted of a master gunner, six old artillerymen, and my detachment. The castle was armed with seven guns.

The Queen's birthday was announced in general orders, and, as usual, the notice was given that every fort in Scotland should fire a salute of twenty-one guns. There existed among the papers in the office a memorandum from the Adjutant-General in Scotland that the guns at Dumbarton Castle were not to be fired, *but on this occasion the said document could not be found,* so I sent for the old master gunner, who informed me that the guns had not been used since the death of His Majesty George IV. But I overcame his scruples by writing an order that a royal salute was to be fired next day. The six patriarchal artillerymen were full of zeal, and we managed in this wise: The detachment of Connaught Rangers was formed up on the top of the rock; the seven old guns were first fired by the ancient gunners, and then my men fired a *feu-de-joie*. This gave time for the venerable artillerymen to load again, and to repeat the fire, an operation which I am thankful to say was effected without any accident, till the twenty-one rounds had been expended.

After giving three hearty cheers for Her Majesty, I dismissed my men to their dinners, and the ancient warriors marched off to their quarters very pleased with their performance. But the authorities did not approve of our loyalty; for I received a reprimand, and an order to pay for the powder expended. Colonel Thorndike, R.A., (late General Thorndike) came to my assistance in this dilemma, and, through his influence, I think I was not called upon to pay anything. As, fortunately, I had blown up nobody, I did not grieve much over the official blowing up, as it was earned in a good cause— loyalty to Her Majesty the Queen.

As the dépôt of the 88th were ordered to proceed from Paisley to Aberdeen, I ceased to be Governor of Dumbarton Castle. We went by train to Stirling, and began there a most enjoyable march. We were received everywhere with open arms, no troops having been along that road since the time of the Peninsular War. The men were not allowed to pay a penny at their billets, and the officers were most kindly welcomed by the hospitable families on whom they were quartered. It was amusing to hear the men giving an account of their adventures as we marched from one place to another.

One day I heard two of them remarking on the fate of a sergeant who had been reduced to the ranks for drunkenness.

'It's sorry I am for Sergeant ———— to be broke by court-martial,' said one.

'Bedad,' replied the other, 'serve him right. He thought he could get drunk, *like an officer !*'

Aberdeen in the year 1844 was a most charming quarter. There was no railway at that period to carry people away to London, or even Edinburgh, and many of the county families came in for the balls at the Assembly Rooms, and were very kind in asking the officers of the 88th to stay in their houses in the county. One of my brother officers had a servant named Casey, who had been quartered at Corfu with the regiment, and was able to play the guitar, and sing Italian airs, the words of which could scarcely be said to belong to any particular language. There was a good theatre at Aberdeen, and Casey was asked to sing between the acts of some play that was having a run. The whole town was placarded with notices that 'a distinguished amateur would sing the "Prayer in Norma."' We officers were greatly interested in this event, and all of us gave Casey different articles of dress, so that he might appear in proper form before the Aberdeen audience. The curtain drew up, and our hero came forward, and sang very well; but, alas, some one had given him whisky before going on the stage, a beverage which naturally took effect on his Irish nature, and instead of retiring gracefully after the conclusion of his song, to our intense disgust, he gave a sort of a screech, and began to dance an Irish jig with the greatest energy. The effect was wonderful, and the gods were delighted. At length the curtain fell, but the noise behind it intimated only too plainly that poor Casey was being taken off to the guard-room, where he passed the night in his borrowed plumes.

I had returned on one occasion to the barracks after a tour of visits in the county to many most agreeable houses. Rather dejected, I was watching Illustrious Tom unpacking my portmanteau. At first I did not take much notice, but very soon my attention was drawn to my servant's performances. First he placed a blotting-book on the table, then he took out another from my portmanteau, and put it on my chest of drawers, and then he placed another somewhere else, and so on, till at last he could find no more vacant resting-places, and he stood in the middle of the room, bearing some resemblance to a sapient owl, with a blotting-book held in his claws.

'What *are* you doing, Tom, with all these blotting-books?' I at length exclaimed.

'Sure,' said the Illustrious, 'I thought ye would be plased. I tuck the different books from the bed-rooms in which yer honour slept. They look well *here*, and they'll nivir miss them *there*.'

As I received his intimation with shouts of laughter and volleys of abuse, Tom drew himself up to attention, faced about, and marched out of my room. My time was fully occupied for several days in finding out to whom the different blotting-books belonged.

A sudden order came for us to leave Scotland and proceed to Ireland. We embarked at Aberdeen in a steamer, and, after a good passage, arrived at Granton, where we landed, and marched through Edinburgh, and thence by train to Glasgow, in which town we were delayed a few days, and then we were taken over to Ireland. While in Glasgow we were made honorary members of the 92nd Highlanders' mess, and at the end of our stay, when we asked for our bills, were told that we were the guests of the regiment.

What a pleasant reminiscence is that of Irish quarters in old times! Everyone was kind and hospitable to the officers of the Army, from the squire in his ancient castle, to the squireen in his more modest house, the property of the latter being often so limited in extent that you could sit on the lodge gate and kick the front door open. We were welcome even to the dwellers in cottages, who, when I entered their lowly cabins, would shout, 'Come in, captin; ye're welcome, sorr;' and, if I did stumble over something in the dark, what did it matter when I was re-assured by the voice of my host saying, 'Niver mind, yer honor, it's only a schlip of a pig?' and truly the repeated grunt, grunt, which followed showed that I had disturbed somewhat unceremoniously the slumbers of that valuable animal, which was fed on the *lavings*, and, when fattened up, 'sowld to pay the rint.' Then the 'quality' were always glad to welcome a young, merry officer, and in the evening one of the 'boys,' who could 'play the fiddle first-rate,' was called in to show his talent, and dance after dance made the night seem too short. What a pleasant time to look back to! Poor old Ireland, with its fearful murders of men and women, and slaying of hounds and cattle, is wofully changed, and I fear the officers of regiments quartered there now do not receive such kindness as I did from high and low. I suppose there was something in the air in those days that made us all so light-hearted, for not a day passed that there was not some fun, and most of the venturesome acts in which we indulged were done for the pure love of sport.

One evening, at Birr, a match, a sort of steeple-chase, was made between two of my brother officers. The night was pitch-dark, and they were to be mounted on their own horses, and to be led into a field about half a mile from the barracks. They were to get over the wall as well as they could, and the first of them who arrived mounted at the mess-room door was to be the winner. They got on their nags and were taken off to the starting-post, where they were invisible to us. We could only hear the word 'Off!' given by the starter. The difficulty was to get over the wall in the dark. One of the riders had a servant, a private in the Rangers, who, of course, was delighted with the sport. We were astounded to hear the voice of this man exclaiming, 'Ride at me, Mr. John, ride at me, sorr!' and all of a sudden a flash burst forth for a moment, and 'Mr. John' made for the light, got over the fence, and rode in triumphant as winner. Pat Casey, his servant, having made a 'slap in the wall,' had then cleverly lit a whole box of lucifers at the place, and thereby enabled his master to get out of the field and come in conqueror.

CHAPTER II.

IN THE WEST INDIES.

CHAPTER II.

WE were quartered for some time at Tralee, a place I shall ever remember with the kindliest feelings for its inhabitants, whose great hospitality was only equalled by their love of good honest sport. On one occasion, when the seniors of the mess were not present, a deal of good-natured chaff had gone on after dinner in the mess-room, where some of the members of the Chute hounds had assembled as guests.

The subject on the tapis was the capabilities of a mare I possessed, which I considered one of the best fencers I ever saw. If you hurried her at her fences she was sure to give you a fall, but leave her alone and nothing in the shape of high banks, for which the country round Tralee was famous, would stop her. The chaff went on, and at length I said,

'I am quite sure the mare would jump this table if asked to do so.'

As many voices proclaimed the impossibility of such a feat, I desired the mess-waiter to tell my groom to saddle the mare and bring her into the mess-room. In a short time the noise of her feet was heard, and as soon as she entered the room, Bayley, a brother officer, jumped up and vaulted on her back. I copy the following narrative from the *New Sporting Magazine*, 1850, page 353.

'Dining at the mess of the "Indomitable Rangers" on the evening of the very last run, I there witnessed an exploit performed which I believe has never been equalled, and I do think never will be excelled. The cloth having been drawn, social converse replaced the cool formality, which is, by some mischance or other, almost the invariable attendant upon dinner-parties; and as might be expected amongst a party where all were sportsmen, and on the evening of a hunting day when a good fox had shown much sport, the topic chosen was the various particulars of the run, and the mode in which each hunter had done its work.

'"I saw you kiss your mother earth twice,

Maxwell," remarked a brother officer; "believe me, that mare of yours is not just the thing," and here from all sides followed many good-humoured criticisms upon the jumping qualities of my friend's prad, to which he (highly delighted at having such an opportunity afforded him "for a lark,") lustily protested the mare should practically reply by then and there popping over the mess-table. The groom being immediately summoned, received in silence, and, as may be imagined, with staring amazement, his master's order "to saddle the mare and bring her in." Many of those present tried to stay the proceedings, but it was now too late; a wilful man, strong in the justice of his cause, would have his way, and in came them are accordingly, much to the consternation of the company assembled, who heard her tramp, tramp, up the boarded passage, knocking out of it the sound of at least a troop of heavy horse.

'Mounted by Mr. Bayley, amidst the glare of wax lights and a blazing coal fire, she actually jumped across the mess-table (a good four feet and a half) without laying an iron on it, and, landing safe on the other side, stood gentle and quiet as 'a lamb upon the floor, under which (as though to increase the hazard of the deed) lay a wine-cellar of from ten to twelve feet deep.'

I remember with great satisfaction that there was not a single bet on the event, and that the mare acquitted herself in the most gallant way, shaking her head and clearing her nostrils, quite pleased after having done what was required of her in the well-lighted mess-room.

The quotation from the *Sporting Magazine* was written and signed by one who, besides being the most pleasant of companions, was a first-rate sportsman. If 'Old Pate' should happen to read these stories of a time long past, I am sure he will recall with pleasure the days gone by.

There was a distinguished cavalry regiment quartered in Ireland during the time our dépôt was wandering about the country. A young cornet joined, who, I believe, was a very good fellow, but so very Irish that his brother officers would not allow him to go out to any parties in the county. Mrs. ——, a very clever woman, was the wife of a gentleman who was proprietor of a large estate near the town where our hero's regiment was stationed. Having previously met the young dragoon, and being delighted with his Milesian remarks, she sent him a pressing invitation to a picnic which she intended giving. After a great deal of trouble he received permission to go, but on the sole condition that he was not to speak a single word the whole time he was there. So off he started, bound by his promise to act the mute.

The scene of the picnic was near a lake, and Mrs. —— managed that the young soldier should accompany a very pretty and amusing girl for a walk before luncheon. Having been told by her hostess that Mr. —— was a most agreeable Irishman, she was very much surprised that, in answer to all her remarks, he only said, ' Ho, ha !' the monotony of which reply terribly bored her. As they came near the lake, however, and were turning a corner, a great swan flew along the water with such a startling noise that it took our poor cornet by surprise, and, forgetting that he was to act the mute, he exclaimed, ' Holy Biddy, look at the goose !' I believe he was never allowed to go to any parties again.

In bygone days valuable horses were often

picked up in unexpected ways. My father, who was a captain in the 23rd Dragoons when 'only sixteen years old, was a wonderfully good judge of a horse. Once, when quartered in Ireland, he saw a man seated on a kish of oysters on the back of a good-looking animal.

'Paddy, will ye sell your horse?' exclaimed my father.

'Bedad I will,' was the reply.

'How much will ye take?' was the next question.

After scratching his head for some time, the man mentioned a price, which my father agreed to give him. The bargain seemed to be coming to an end, when the Irishman said,

'Och, tear-an-ages, I forgot the oysters!' which difficulty was met by the would-be purchaser declaring,

'I'll buy you, your horse, and your oysters.'

Whether the man was kept I do not know, but the horse and the oysters became my father's property, and most probably a merry supper-party disposed of the latter to commemorate the event. The new purchase was named 'Paddy Oysters,' and an acquisition he proved, for he won several plates in Ireland, and was well known everywhere. My father became major of the 23rd Dragoons, and then raised a battalion of the Cameronians, 26th Regiment, hoping to get the lieutenant-colonelcy of a cavalry regiment, as he had always served in that branch of the service; but the Duke of York told him he must command the corps he had raised, a high honour to him, and he went out to Spain as lieutenant-colonel of the 26th Cameronians, which formed part of the force under Sir John Moore, a personal friend of his own. So my father went to the wars, and took Paddy Oysters as his charger. At the battle of Corunna his left arm was shattered by a cannon ball, and he was hurried off on board a transport, where the wounded limb was taken out at the socket. Alas! poor Paddy Oysters! The order was given that all horses were to be shot to prevent them falling into the hands of the French; so the gallant charger was condemned to die. The colonel's groom would allow no one to touch his master's faithful steed. Although the enemy was approaching, and no doubt there was a good deal of hurry and excitement, he waited for orders, which were given, and Paddy Oysters fell dead on the beach. These particulars were given me by my father as well as by my uncle, who was present at the time.

A soldier's life is one of continual change. I suppose, among its many charms, that of uncertainty is one of the greatest. We were quartered at Tralee, and in the full enjoyment of all the sport and hospitality which are the distinguishing features of that most charming quarter. I well remember one evening; we had had a first-rate run with the Chute foxhounds, and it was late before I got back to my quarters. My room looked very comfortable, Illustrious Tom having made a fine fire of turf and coal mixed. Everything seemed so pleasant, and I daresay the thought entered my mind what a jolly season was before me. There were some letters on the table. One official-looking document I left to the last, believing it referred to some court-martial duty. However, at length I opened it and found a note from my commanding officer, regretting that he was obliged to forward the enclosed to me; which was an order from the Horse Guards for Captain Maxwell to proceed to join the head-quarters of the 88th Connaught

Rangers at Barbadoes, West Indies. So my Irish campaign was over, and I had to say farewell to Tralee and all its charms, and to leave behind me not only my brothers-in-arms, but, among other treasures, Illustrious Tom and his fat wife.

The steamer started from Southampton. We touched at Madeira, and, after a prosperous passage, cast anchor at Barbadoes.

The head-quarters of the Connaught Rangers were ordered to Trinidad, four companies under my command to the Island of Grenada, and another detachment under Captain Bayley to St. Vincent. The 88th had suffered fearfully from that awful disease, yellow fever. Our much beloved Colonel Ormsby Phibbs had fallen a victim to it, and many men had lost their lives. Yellow Jack left us the moment we sailed from Barbadoes, and during the two years I was quartered at Grenada we had no hospital to speak of, and only one man died, a poor man who fell a victim to new rum. We got up a race meeting, open to all the islands in the West Indies. Captain Astley, 66th Regiment, brought a horse down from Barbadoes named Creole, and won everything with it. He was a very nice fellow, and we were all glad at his success, as it showed much sporting spirit to bring a horse to run at such a distance from where his regiment was quartered. The stakes he had won were all in dollars, and the bag he had to carry away was so large that Captain Astley asked me, as secretary and treasurer, to have the money sent to him through the Colonial Bank at Grenada. We said farewell to this gallant officer on board the steamer which was to take him back to Barbadoes. He was in great spirits, and apparently in excellent health. But, alas! the return steamer from Barbadoes, in a very few days, brought a letter from the paymaster of the 66th Regiment, telling the sad story that Astley was dead; yellow fever having carried him off.

Among the fair places of the earth there is none fairer than the Island of Grenada. The Carenage and town of St. Georges are situated at the foot of high hills covered with trees. The road winds up a green avenue, and gradually ascends to Fort Mathew, where four companies of the Rangers were quartered. What a view there was from the verandah of my rooms! The town of St. Georges appeared to consist of toy buildings, half encircling the harbour, and, far beyond, miles and miles of sea. In the day time everything was bright and lively : the balmy trade winds blew fresh and perfumed; the night, when every tree and bush was lit up by sparkling fireflies, appeared calm and peaceful; rare flowers seemed to grow uncared for—flowers which at home would have been highly valued and carefully tended. Fruit is plentiful, and pine-apples are very fine; a brilliant purple blossom, resembling the single bell of the hyacinth, opens from each of the diamond-shaped divisions of the fruit itself, which when young is of the same rich hue, surrounded by a crest of pink-corded leaves, and protected all round by others much larger and broader, with saw-like edges and spiked points. The pine-apple, as it ripens, loses its beautiful and fresh appearance ; the purple changes to pale strawberry, and the leaves become green. It is placed in ice, and sliced; and there cannot be anything more delicious than this juicy fruit when the sun is high and the trade wind has failed.

It would take pages to describe the various

dishes a gourmet might revel in at Grenada; turtle in every way, pepper-pot, and land-crabs. I can only recommend those who have large yachts to go to the West Indies for a cruise. Land-crab catching was a very picturesque scene. These creatures, which live in holes near the sea, are strangely ugly. At night we used to sally forth, attended by crowds of niggers, and proceed to an inlet from the sea, on the shore of which the manchineel-trees grow. If you take refuge from the rain underneath the shade of these treacherous shrubs, your face and hands become blistered all over. The ground is full of holes where the land-crabs dwell. Fascinated by the torch-light (which each native carries), they come out, and are seized by the expert watcher. These crabs are supposed to be foul feeders, and when caught they are placed in barrels, and fed on meal for many days before they are cooked for the table. Another exciting sport was turtle turning. The natives would watch a turtle com-ing out of the water to lay her eggs, and, before she got back to the sea, would intercept her, and turn her over on her back, in which posi-tion a turtle is quite helpless. Having marked the spot where the eggs were deposited, they went there, and generally found an enormous quantity. These eggs when boiled have a skin like parchment. One becomes in time quite clever at opening them. The way a West Indian gourmet eats them was always a wonder to me, though I became pretty expert at it after some practice.

My brother officer, Lee Steere, and myself were greatly interested in the race-meeting before mentioned. Both of us had horses to run, and we had to train them ourselves; so we discovered an old house near the race-course—which we called Jockey Lodge—and there we came and lived occasionally before the races. The house was very old, and the wooden flooring quite out of repair. I was attacked in it by some very disagreeable symptoms. I suppose I had walked on the floor in my bed-room without slippers; for one morning I felt the most maddening itching in one of my toes, so I shouted for my servant Seeley, who was a first-rate attendant, and asked him what could be the matter. He and his wife had both been slaves who had been freed by Colonel Tidy, I think, of the 14th Regiment. The colonel had given Seeley a watch with an inscription on it at the time when he made him a free man. Whenever anything out of the common happened, Seeley would roll his eyes, and grin from ear to ear, showing his white teeth, and looking the embodiment of black mischief. Having examined my foot, he almost shouted with delight.

'Yah! yah! Massa got jigger toe. Yah! yah!'

I did not appreciate his mirth and laughter.

'What am I to do, you horrible old rascal?' I exclaimed.

Seeley bent nearly double, and with his hands on the front of his thighs, assumed the attitude of long-stop at cricket, and continued to give expression to his sense of enjoyment. 'Yah! yah! ho! ho!' But at length he became quiet, and proceeded to business. Taking a needle, he began to scrape away at my toe, nearly driving me mad. Suddenly he exclaimed, ' Hi haw!' like a donkey braying, and then he appeared to force the needle gently into my foot, and brought out at the end of it a little bag, which he held up with a triumphant look; for this was the jigger, which had laid its eggs in my toe, and which, if allowed to remain, would have been attended with most serious consequences.

I had a thirty-ton cutter, in which I made several expeditions. Once I went to Trinidad, where the head-quarters of the 88th were stationed. I do not remember how long we took to go there, but I recall with pleasure that delightful sail over a calm sea, a favouring breeze filling our sails. As we cut through the water, flying fish darted here and there, either in fear or in play; the nautilus floated gracefully, dolphins leaped, and sometimes the horrid fin of a shark following our track might be seen. It is long ago since all this happened, and I can only trust to my memory, but I think the barracks where the Connaught Rangers were stationed must have been the very abode of fever. The mosquitoes were intolerable, and the heat intense. Lord Harris was governor then, and his gardens were beautiful. I well remember the luxurious marble bath in his grounds. My colonel, the late Sir H. Shirley, gave me a room in his quarters, and in the morning he awoke me to show a huge tarantula, as big as the back of my hand, which a gunner had found in his boot as he was about to pull it on.   I also saw a centipede, which the assistant-surgeon of the regiment was preserving, so long that in a common-sized havanna cigar-box it could not be placed without almost doubling it. So my recollections of Trinidad are a conglomeration of tarantulas, mosquitoes, centipedes, iced champagne, and a hearty welcome.

My regiment went from the West Indies to Halifax, Nova Scotia.   We changed from almost perpetual sunshine to a land where snow lay on the ground for months.   When we landed, I well remember how fresh and beautiful everything looked.   I had been accustomed for some years to see for the most part only the negro women, who, although possessing figures like graceful ebony statues, that showed to the finest advantage as they walked erect and firm, bearing their purchases from market on a tray carried on the top of their heads, still their faces, as a rule, were ugly, and always black.   How surpassingly beautiful we thought the women of Halifax, with their dazzling complexions, who came to welcome the wild Irishmen ; and further acquaintance showed that their beauty was only equalled by their frank and gentle ways.   The year we remained at Halifax is a memory never to be effaced. The venerable and rickety old wooden barracks, which had been condemned during the time the Duke of Kent was in Nova Scotia, was burnt to the ground when the 88th and 38th Regiments occupied it as quarters. The conflagration was a grand sight, which we would willingly have dispensed with, as the Connaught Rangers never received any compensation for the mess napery and other valuables lost in that magnificent bonfire.

The mention of land-crab catching in Grenada recalls to me the lobster-spearing at Halifax, a sport which was carried on at night. In the bows of the boat large fires were kept burning. Standing ready, the sportsman holds in his grasp a trident, which is not pointed, but is like a huge pair of tweezers. The lobsters are seen crawling beneath the clear water. A sudden dart is made with the trident, the tweezers open, and seize the prey, which is hauled on board and thrown among others in the bottom of the boat. Many dozens are caught in this way, and the scene is very exciting when there are several boats, the fires in them looking strange and weird-like.

If I were to begin recalling old times at Halifax, with its sleigh club in winter and the flowers of its summer, I fear I should become very wearisome. When my regiment was quartered in Nova Scotia, we got a bear, about the size of a small donkey, which became a great favourite. The order came for us to return home in the troop-ship *Resistance*, commanded by Captain Bradshaw. Great was our consternation when that officer issued a proclamation that only a certain number of pets, and no bears, should be allowed on board. We all vowed that the bear was not to be left behind, and a clever plan to smuggle it on board was hit upon by two of my brother officers. As there were many casks to be hoisted on board, chloroform was administered to our bear, and he was packed in one of them. As it was going to be hoisted in the air, the captain asked,

'What's in that big barrel?'

The Ranger, who was seeing it elevated, answered, promptly,

'The warm clothing of the regiment, sorr,' and being asked by a comrade why he said so, he observed, with a wink, 'Begorra, I thought the ould Tartar moight see the fur through the bunghole of the cask and smell—a bear!'

The sailors were delighted and helped to stow our favourite away, and I believe the captain never knew anything about it till we had been some time at sea, and then he pretended to have been cognizant of the fact all along. Our bear was with us at Parkhurst Barracks, and was always in a friendly disposition with all. A young fellow dined at our mess, and I suppose drank too much champagne, for he was discovered peacefully reposing beside the bear in its kennel.

The 38th Regiment brought home two bears, very fine, large animals. A child was playing with them and got a hug, which killed the poor little thing. Down came an official from the Horse Guards with orders that all regimental bears were to be destroyed; we gave ours, however, to the Zoo, where it lived in the pit and was fed with buns by children. Round its neck was a brass collar with 'Connaught Rangers' engraved on it. I do not know its further history.

CHAPTER III.

ENGLAND AND THE CONTINENT.

CHAPTER III.

ON our arrival in England we disembarked at Chatham and marched to Canterbury, where we were quartered for some months. The 17th Lancers, who occupied the cavalry barracks, were one of the most hospitable and pleasant corps I ever met; many of them have passed away, many of them fell in the glorious charge of Balaclava, but at the time of which I write they formed a gathering of the finest specimens of the light dragoon.

When the leave time came round I went to Paris. The late emperor was then President of the French Republic, and enjoyment seemed the order of the day. The balls of the Tuileries were most amusing; all officers were in uniform, and the dress of the 17th Lancers of that day, several of whom were present at one of these balls, was universally admired. I went in the tight coatee with epaulettes which was an infantry officer's costume at that time, and no doubt thought myself very fine; but my vanity received a shock when a French lady passed, and, looking towards me, said to her friend, 'Ma foi, c'est un véritable Rosbif!' We were received with great civility by the officers of the artillery quartered at Vincennes, who invited us to pay them a visit, which we did a day or two after the ball. Nothing could exceed the friendliness of these French gunners. We dined with them in a café, as they had no mess, and I remember the great event was the 'plum poudin,' the very remembrance of which fills my mind with horror. The excitement of the Frenchmen was intense when a large soup tureen was placed on the table. 'Ah, le voilà! Le plum poudin! Ah, oh!' When the cover was removed a mass of liquid horrors was brought to view, among which a bottle of cognac was poured and then lighted. This fearful decoction was ladled out into soup plates, and with anxious eyes our friends gazed on us as we began to eat. I suppose the brandy saved us, but we certainly endangered our lives for the honour of our country.

When we were leaving, these kindly-disposed fellows insisted on paying our cab hire to Paris, and we had the greatest difficulty in preventing them doing so. We were anxious to give them some return for their civility, so the lancers and myself resolved to ask them to dinner at the Rocher de Cancale. A note was therefore despatched requesting the pleasure of their company. A reply came to me from one of them, a nice young fellow called Joubert, begging us to postpone the entertainment for a week. Of course this was complied with, and when the week had elapsed we had a very jolly party. Joubert accounted for the delay which had been requested, which was owing, as he said, to the fact that we had honoured them with our presence in plain clothes, and, as they had nothing but uniform, they had to get mufti made! This was quite touching by its simple courtesy.

We had a great deal of fun during our stay in Paris. On our first arrival my friends, the lancers, asked me to order dinner at the 'Trois Frères,' which was in existence then. I was determined to have a good dinner; but I had forgotten Parisian ways, having been absent for so long in the West Indies and America. Anyway, I ordered a portion for each person. I think we numbered eight; so there were eight soups, eight fish, eight of each entrée, &c., and the room seemed hardly large enough to contain our various *plats*. How we did laugh and enjoy ourselves! With one exception, I am now the only one left of that merry party.

My leave was drawing to a close, so I left Paris, where every moment had been so occupied. I had not done much in letter-writing, and was, therefore, quite ignorant of regimental news. On arriving at Canterbury, I got a fly, and ordered the driver to take me to the barracks; but, on reaching the infantry lines, I was surprised to find all in darkness, although it was only about half-past seven in the evening.

At length an 88th man came up to the carriage in which I was seated.

‘What's become of everybody?’ I exclaimed.

‘Well, sorr, they're all gone; a sudden order came, and they're gone, except just a few to give over the barracks.’

'Gone—where to?' I asked.

After a time he replied, 'They're gone, sorr, to some island; but I disremember the name.'

With this very unsatisfactory information, I told cabby to drive me to the 'Fountain Hotel,' where I was told that the regiment had lfet for the Isle of Wight.

Parkhurst Barracks was occupied by only one battalion, the 88th, and the four company dépôt of the Cameronians. What delightful quarters the Isle of Wight was in these days! There was no railway then in the island; a four-horse coach plied between Newport and Ryde, and the drive was most enjoyable. The pretty little villages have now become staring towns. It is difficult to find a retired nook in the noisy country now all built over.

The officers of the 88th received the greatest hospitality from everyone in the Isle of Wight. The numbers were not overwhelming, there being few red-coats at the barracks. The private soldiers also were most kindly treated by the inhabitants of this charming island. It is a strange fact that at home in Britain, because a man wears a red coat and is liable to a greater punishment for drunkenness than a civilian, kind-hearted men consider themselves bound to offer him a dram, and even press him to take it, while to another class of men they would only wish 'God speed.' When my regiment was quartered at Parkhurst Barracks, an election took place, and the usually quiet town of Cowes was very excited. I had been asked to dinner there by a very hospitable host, and a married brother officer offered me a seat in his carriage. The party was a very pleasant one, and the cheers of the successful candidate's supporters were distinctly heard every now and then.

When we were leaving, my friend saw that his coachman, a private soldier, had been drinking success to the newly-elected member—in other words, was very drunk, so he whispered to me to get inside with his wife, and that he would drive. The lady, however, was not to be deceived by remarks about the pleasures of smoking a cigar and driving home by moonlight. She soon exclaimed,

'I am sure there is something wrong,' and at this moment coachee made a tremendous lurch. 'The servant is drunk. He will knock my husband off the box. Oh! Captain Maxwell, do, do something.'

What could I do to pacify this kind lady, whose husband was my dearest friend? I was in a dreadful quandary. A bright idea came to the anxious wife.

'Oh, Captain Maxwell, will you hold the man on to the box?'

So I let down the front window, and with considerable difficulty got hold of some part of the horrid man's dress, and so pretended to keep him steady. The tipsy wretch made a horrible lurch, and, giving his master a poke in the ribs, said, in a tone half jovial, half sad,

'Meejor, the missus is pulling my tail!'

We left the Isle of Wight, and, after being quartered for some months at Portsmouth, proceeded to join the camp at Chobham. How much we enjoyed that bloodless campaign, and how absurdly proud of ourselves we all were! The Connaught Rangers were composed of as fine a body of men as could be mustered anywhere, well seasoned soldiers, full of loyalty to the Queen, and imbued with a thorough knowledge of their duties, which it takes many years to learn, and thus enable a private to become a good non-commissioned officer. In two years from that time how few remained alive! Most of them repose in death on the heights of Sebastopol, where the wild flowers cover their honoured graves. But Chobham was the first camp which had been formed for many years, and we all enjoyed it very much. It was amusing to watch the curiosity displayed by civilians. I have often seen visitors to the camp walk through our mess-kitchen, and horrify our cook by taking the lids off some of his most cherished pots to see what we were to have for dinner.

I remember one day, after a long field-day in the warm sun, going to my tent, throwing my-self into an arm-chair, and very nearly falling asleep, when I heard a whispering going on at the entrance, which was gently opened, when a pretty face peeped in, and I heard the remark made, 'He is asleep,' but, like the celebrated weasel, I had an eye open. One peculiar feature of Chobham at that time was, that friends who had previously ignored one's existence all of a sudden became greatly interested in our welfare, especially about luncheon time. The camp at

Chobham was the first opportunity many of us had of seeing regiments combined together in brigades and divisions. It was a grand picnic, and was the melodious overture to the great tragedy of the Crimean War.

We were visited by royal personages, by soldiers, sailors, lawyers, and clergymen. The celebrated Dr. Cumming once addressed the men. I remember some of his remarks:

'I am a man of peace, but, if anyone tried to knock me down, I would do all I could to floor him first.'

The chaplain-general preached a sermon. He said,

'The last time he had seen such a gathering of soldiers, he himself had taken an active part, for he was then an officer under Wellington.'

Though no one was certain then that there would be war, yet there was a sulphurous vapour impregnating the air, which the most peaceable inhaled, and the next year the Crimean campaign came on.

After leaving Chobham, we were sent to the manufacturing districts. The head-quarters was stationed at Bury, in Lancashire, and the left wing, to which I belonged, was sent to Ashton-under-Line. The cotton-spinners were most hospitable to us. I have a very kindly remembrance of a Mr. Harrison, whose house was in the neighbourhood of our barracks, and who showed me the greatest kindness. But the plot was thickening, and the order came for the Connaught Rangers to embark for the East. The whole of Ashton turned out to see us march away. The streets were decorated, and as the colours were carried past every head was uncovered. One man, however, standing near the hotel in the street through which we passed, did not take off his hat. A young fellow went up to him, and, I suppose, told him to uncover, but ho refused to do so. I heard him say: 'No, I won't.' The next moment he was lying on the ground, the young fellow having hit him right between the eyes, and knocked him down. As we proceeded onward, an old woman knelt, and in a loud voice blessed the colours.

When we arrived in Liverpool, we were halted near the Exchange, and the mayor made a speech, which was received with great cheering. The ships in the harbour were gaily decorated with flags, and crowds of people shouted and cheered. On the 4th of April, 1854, the Connaught Rangers embarked on board the *Niagara*, one of Cunard's finest steamers, on which we were most sumptuously entertained. On arriving at Constantinople we asked for our bill, and were informed we were guests of the Cunards. We subscribed, and presented the captain with a watch.

Our passage out was a very prosperous one. A calm sea prevailed nearly all the time. Our band played often on deck, and in the bright moonlight the men sat in groups and sang merrily. I still possess some of their cheery ditties.

LOVE, FAREWELL.

' Now, brave boys, we're bound for marchin',
    Both to Portingale and Spain;
Drums are batin', colours flyin',
    And the divil a back we'll come agin.
      So, love, farewell!

' Eighty-eighty and Inniskillen,
    Boys that's able, boys that's willin',
Faugh-a-ballagh and County Down,
    Stand by the Harp, and stand by the Crown.
      So, love, farewell!

' The colonel cries, "Boys, are yez ready?"
    " We're at your back, sir, firm and steady,

Our pouches filled with ball and pouther,
And a firelock sloped on every shoulther."
So, love, farewell!

' Och, Judy dear, ye're young and tender,
When I'm away ye'll not surrender,
But hould out like an ancient Roman,
And I'll make you—an honest woman.
So, love, farewell!

' Och, Judy, should I die in glory,
In the papers ye'll read my awful story;
But I'm so bothered with yer charms,
I'd rather die within your arms.
So, love, farewell!'

I must give another specimen, which, if not very well spelt, is otherwise a proof of the loyalty of a gallant soldier, who afterwards fell at Sebastopol. I copy the whole as given to me on board the *Niagara*.

'A soldier that is bound for this late war, and who goes with the most gratified assurance of coming home again with the head of the Disturber of Europe; or, dying like a soldier in the field, and with the heart of a real true subject, he says to his comrades:—

COME TO THE DANOBE.

(Composed by Private Edward Murphy, Light Company, 88th Regiment.)

' Our allies to joine, my boys,
The English and Frinch
Is going to combine, my boys.

We'll fight till the last,
And no mortal we'll spare, my boys.
What better fun could you ask
Than chasing the bear, my boys ?
Now let us with curage
Enter the field, my boys,
And the bigoted tyrent
We'll make him yield, my boys ;
And out of the Principalities
We'll make him elope ;
We'll show him more play
Then he got at Synope.
Come, then, come to the Danobe.
For the Rangers at present
Is wiling to fight, I know,
And with Colonel Shirley no
Dangers they'll slight, I know.
May he lead them on to fame,
As Wallace before has don,
And live to command us
Untill the battle's won.
Then come to the Danobe,
And our officers all
The right sort of chaps are they,
Comboyned one and all,
And ready for the fray,
We'll conquer or die,
And may we all live to see
The Rushins to fly,
Beat both on land and sea.'

On arriving at Gallipoli, we received orders to proceed on to Constantinople. A boat was upset close to our steamer, and one of the Turks took refuge in the paddle-wheel! Most fortunately, he was not killed. When he came on board, we gave him dry clothes, and, as it was the men's dinner hour, they offered him some pork. His face would have made a good picture. I mention this as the first mistake made by our soldiers in their dealings with Mohammedans.

We anchored near Scutari, between the Sultan's seraglio and the opposite shore, and in the afternoon we disembarked, and marched into Scutari Barracks, a fine building capable of containing six thousand men. My company, numbering over one hundred, were all in one room. The quarters told off for two subalterns and myself consisted of one large room, lighted by three windows, in front of which was an ottoman with pillows. Cleanliness was not the order of the day, so there were many inhabitants besides ourselves. Our view was not enlivening, as we looked out on the Scutari burying ground, where tall, sombre cypress-trees waved sadly over the tombs of thousands of Mahomet's followers. In the evening we went for a walk, and, seeing a crowd, we made towards it and found two Turks stripped to the skin, their only garment being a kind of bathing drawers. They were smeared with oil and were engaged wrestling. The wrestlers were not a very pleasing sight, but the *entourage* was most amusing. Here was a Connaught Ranger in his neat red coat and white belt, without any weapon at all; there a wild warrior of some eastern tribe, armed to the teeth with formidable pistols and curved scimitar. There were women covered up to the eyes, but the eyes were soft and bright, Greeks with long pipes, Turks in green turbans, and Turks in white—a strange and animated scene.

A good story was told of a gallant colonel commanding a most distinguished regiment. He had been given quarters in the Sultan's wing in Scutari Barracks. A pasha came to pay him an official visit, and, I suppose, approached with reverence the apartments sacred in his estimation. He took off his slippers at the door and entered the room, when, horror of horrors! what did he see?—the said colonel occupied frying pork in a dispatcher on the Sultan's table.

A brother officer and myself crossed one day by the steamer which plied from Scutari to

Galata, and there hired a caique. We were bound for the sweet waters of Europe. We were taken up the Golden Horn, and then floated past green hills and picturesque-looking cottages. All round us were hundreds of gilded caiques laden with handsome women in glittering attire, and boats whose Greek crews sang in wild chorus. As we proceeded onward the river became narrow, and we arrived at the sweet waters of Europe. It was a fairy scene. Graceful forms in lovely dresses were dotted here and there on the green grass under the shade of the trees, very transparent veils concealing their faces, their long fringed eyes beaming upon us, for the unbelievers were in high favour at that time. We passed also stately Turks, gay Frenchmen, steady-looking Britons, and wonderful Cinderella coaches. A gilded carriage approached, drawn by four black horses, covered with silver trappings; this was followed by a line of other gilded coaches surrounded by armed blacks. A lovely woman glittering with diamonds, her face barely concealed by the thin gauze she wore, was in the stately equipage. This was the Sultan's wife. In the third carriage following hers was seated a most beautiful girl, by whose charms my brother officer was quite struck. Though he was jostled by the armed blacks, pushed by the escort, knocked by the Turks, he still kept as close as possible to No. 3 carriage. There are many old women at the valley of sweet waters who sell bouquets. One came near and offered some flowers to my brother-officer, who took them, and, watching his opportunity, presented them to this Nourmahal. She smiled and placed them in her bosom, and, taking a rose from the bouquet, held it towards my friend, and then pressed the flower to her lips, on perceiving which the armed blacks began to swagger offensively. The escort of lancers closed up, and, as the carriages were moving away, she rolled her handkerchief up and threw it at my bewildered friend. She then held a looking-glass towards him and pressed it in her arms, thus ending the romance as far as I know, for the gilded coaches and prancing escort all moved on and gradually faded from our sight.

CHAPTER IV.

IN TURKEY AND THE CRIMEA.

CHAPTER IV.

ON the 29th of May, 1854, we embarked on board the *Cambria*, and on the 30th arrived at Varna, where we encamped for a few days. On the 5th of June we changed our ground. Our tents were pitched on a height between two lakes. The hills all around us were covered with young trees in beautiful foliage, and on our right was a valley, through which a broad river flowed. The green hills were dotted everywhere with white tents, and curling smoke was stealing out of the woods from many a bivouac fire. It was an enchanting sight. Some of our baggage horses had been stolen, but a few had been recovered. As there was a difficulty, however, in recognising them, Sir George Brown, the general of the light division, issued an order that each animal belonging to the different regiments forming the light division should have some identifying mark, so that, if any of them were stolen, their recovery might be facilitated.

The adjutant of the Connaught Rangers, Arthur Maule, gave orders to his batman to have his initials burnt on his horse's hind-quarters. I suppose Paddy did not know what initials meant, for Maule, on proceeding with his batman to inspect his nag, found B. R. beautifully clipped and burnt on the charger's hind-quarters.

'What does B. R. mean?' said the astonished officer. 'My initials are A. M.'

'Arrah, sure, sir,' replied the rather offended groom, 'B. R. stands for British Army.'

The peasantry were much alarmed at our approach at first; but they very soon found out that we were willing to pay freely for the produce of their farms, and in process of time they actually walked through our camp shouting out what they had for sale. One poor man I heard crying out, in a very loud voice, 'Bono Johnny. Bono *bad* eggs!' the result, no doubt, of some wag's tuition. Colonel Sanders, of the 19th Regiment, and myself rode out one day to forage among the villages, whose inhabitants were generally pleased to provide us with whatever they possessed for a consideration.

This day we had been very successful, and our appearance would have surprised those at home, who think officers of the Army the most luxurious of men. Colonel Sanders had become possessor of several fresh eggs, which he placed in his pockets. I was the proud owner of a duck and two hens, which were put in front of me on the baggage pony I was riding. We got on very well at first; but my duck became obstreperous, and the hens struggled, so my nag began to kick, and roused Colonel Sanders' charger to do likewise—alas! for the colonel's coat, where now the pomp and circumstance of glorious war ? 'Oh! the eggs are all smashed!' was the colonel's most distressing announcement. We rode into camp very curious specimens of the British soldier. Sanders went away to pass a *mauvais quart d'heure* with his batman, and I was received with joy by my servant, Hopkins, who expressed his delight in the following forcible, if not very elegant terms :

'Hurroo! here's fowls. I've had nothing to

rub the sweat off my teeth but stale bread. Hurroo!'

The time passed in Bulgaria by the light division would have been a long continued picnic had not pestilence come upon us, and cholera visited our camp in its most cruel form. It is very sad to recall to one's memory that beautiful spot which simply by a change of wind was altered from a paradise to a place where death in one of its most horrid forms reigned supreme. We changed our ground very often, but the hideous demon followed us wherever we went, and we welcomed the order when issued for the light division to march to Varna, there to embark.

One cold, raw evening, when cholera was at its worst, several of us were sitting in my tent drinking hot rum and water. The sergeant of my company came to make some report, and I offered him some hot grog, which he accepted. With the greatest care I mixed the drink, and gave it to him, while he made some kindly remark as he drank it off, and then went away. Some one else, coming into the tent soon after, was also invited to 'liquor up.' The mug in which the sergeant's grog had been was still on the table, and the little that was left looked so curious that I put my lips to it, and was terribly distressed to find that I had used salt instead of sugar in concocting it. The great fear came over me that it would make the sergeant feel sick, and that he might fancy he had taken cholera; so I sent for him, and, when he came, I told him of my mistake. His answer surprised me; for he said he knew it was salt from the taste.

'But, sergeant, was it not very horrid?' I exclaimed.

'Well, sir, it was rather nauseous,' he replied.

'Why did you drink it?' I asked.

'I did not like to let on that I knew it, as you had kindly given me the drink,' was the astounding reply.

On our march to Varna, we were encamped on the ground which had been vacated by the 79th Highlanders. Our tents were pitched, but great difficulty had been experienced in getting the sick settled in camp, and the doctors had been most terribly overworked. When the detachment of the 88th Regiment were quartered at Grenada in the West Indies, I saw mentioned in the *Gazette* the appointment to the Connaught Rangers of a man with a very curious name, Shegog. This name haunted me, and I never took up a newspaper without reading that Shegog was appointed assistant-surgeon to the 88th. The steamer arrived early one morning at Grenada, and I was wondering what news had come from England when my servant announced, 'Dr. Shegog.' The doctor was a curious-looking man, with very prominent eyes, and, when he put his hat on, it was always very far back on his head; but, when we came to know him, we found that there never was a truer man than 'Old Shay;' no warmer heart ever beat than his. He accompanied the regiment to Nova Scotia; and after being quartered, on our return home, with me at Ashton-under-Line, he embarked with the 88th on board the *Niagara*, to proceed to Turkey, in April, 1854.

When cholera attacked the light division in Bulgaria, Dr. Shegog never flagged in his attentions to the sick, while he took but little care of himself. The hospital tent was a fearful place to visit. The poor men were lying on the ground writhing in agony; crying out to be rubbed in accents most pitiful to hear. Others were too far gone to feel pain—their last hour was nearly come. 'Old Shay' was everywhere, and doing all in his power for the suffering soldiers. The Roman Catholic priest might be seen kneeling beside the dying men whispering hope to their passing spirits.

The joyous order came at last to move to Varna for embarkation. The news came like a tonic, and the weary men seemed to gain strength at once. Our brigade marched away, and we were full of joyful anticipations. Dr. Shegog had been so occupied looking after the sick that he had no time to think of himself. The poor fellow's tent was pitched, but he had no dinner to eat. Steevens, Browne, and I messed together, and, as our repast was over, nothing remained. Shegog came to my tent, and asked if we could give him something to eat, but we had not one scrap left. He was told there was lots of brandy, to which he was welcome at any time. He thanked us, but said he wanted something to eat, and at that moment Maule, the adjutant, appeared, and said, 'Come along, Old Shay, I have something cold in my tent,' and so he went away. Next morning, poor, kind-hearted Shegog died of cholera. A man came to me, and told me that the doctor was very ill. When I saw him, all pain was over, and he soon sank to rest. He was buried under the shade of a tree. Who knows the place of his grave now? But what matter? Wherever he may be laid, it is the resting-place of a true and honest worker who lost his life in helping the sick and weary.

As we returned to the camp from Shegog's funeral, one of my brothers-in-arms said he felt very unwell. We cheered him up as well as we could, but as the night went on he became really ill, and, in the morning, our surgeon passed my tent, and said, 'Mackie has got cholera.'

The regiment was preparing to proceed on the march to Varna, for we had nearly reached our destination, and our chief, Shirley, proposed that Mackie should be left till later in the day— under charge of a guard—but, as he decided to accompany the battalion, a stretcher was made as comfortable as possible for him, and he was carried by some men of his company. On approaching Varna, he asked them to lower him down to the ground, which they had no sooner done than poor Mackie expired.

Our embarkation at Varna was effected without difficulty. Our vessel, which was towed by a steamer, formed one of that magnificent fleet of men-of-war and transports that covered the Black Sea for miles. When night came on, the scene was marvellous to look upon; light after light shining in the far distance over the calm sea. Sometimes the sea resembled a large harbour full of vessels at anchor, then it assumed the appearance of long streets in some vast town, but all was silent, and filled our minds with awe.

The light division landed at Old Fort in the Crimea. There was no opposition from the Russians, not one of whom was visible, except some Cossacks on a distant hill. We marched only a few miles from where we had disembarked, and halted in what appeared to be a stubble-field, but, as darkness had come on, it was difficult to know where we were. While we were in this state of perplexity, it began to rain. I was dressed in, I believe, the identical coat in which I had appeared at the Tuileries ball, which was uncomfortable for even a drawing-room, but quite unsuited for a wet night in a ploughed field. For hours the rain continued, and we were all wet through. The men, in the morning, managed to light a fire, and one of them brought me a mug of hot rum and water, which was most delicious. What kindly fellows these private soldiers were in those by-gone days! I daresay they are the same now, but I only testify to what they were then, from my experience of them.

In a day or two we got our tents and were comparatively comfortable. One night some firing was heard, which was taken up by the whole line of sentries. What an excitement it was! Stevens and I shared the same tent, sleeping on the ground, without light of any kind, in total darkness. When the hurly-burly began— the buglers sounding the alarm, followed by the assembly—we both jumped up, and struggled to get our shakoes, which, of course, had hid themselves. Scrambling in the dark, our two heads came bang against each other, and nearly floored us both, but at length, after a fall over the tent ropes, we reached my company. One of our staff-sergeants was an excitable man. It is reported of him that on that night he rushed about with a drawn sword in a most frantic way, and nearly knocked over a bugler, who, seeing this wild man rushing at him, fell on his knees, exclaiming, in terrified accents,

'Spare me, spare me, I'm a frind!'

This was our first scare in the Crimea, and was caused by some horses having got loose and surprised the sentries.

The story of the Crimean War has been told so often that I am not going to inflict the oft-repeated tale on my friends, but only mention a few facts which are not universally known.

It was the day before the battle of the Alma, when one of my brother officers was taken very ill with symptoms of cholera. There was a small house, I think a post-house, near our bivouac, and my friend took refuge there. He had not been long established in these humble quarters when a staff officer came and informed him he was sorry he must turn him out, but that Lord Raglan's head-quarters had been fixed there, and that his lordship was then approaching.

Lord Raglan came up during this conversation, and, on being informed of the case, insisted that my brother officer should remain undisturbed where he was, had a chair brought in to make him more comfortable, and, later in the day, with his one hand, carried a bowl of soup to my suffering friend, and this was on the night before the battle of the Alma. Lord Raglan showed in many acts what a kind heart was his. Later, when the siege of Sebastopol was progressing, Nat Stevens and I were sitting in our closed tent, enjoying a fire. Nat was an inventive genius, and had found an old funnel lying about, and had made a kind of a chimney, through which escaped some of the smoke, that was caused by a few damp roots burning in a very primitive fire-place. We were actually weeping for joy, as a great deal of smoke refused to leave us. It was snowing heavily outside the tent, when a voice was heard shouting. With many exclamations of disgust Nat opened the tent. A figure on a horse, all alone, was barely visible in the snow.

'What are you burning?' asked the rider. 'I see you have a fire by the smoke.'

'Roots,' answered Nat.

'Remember, do not burn charcoal; an officer of

the 97th Regiment has lost his life by doing so,'
said Lord Raglan, for he it was, who, bent on
deeds of kindly care, rode, unlike the French
generals, unattended by any staff, his visits to the
camp thus remaining unknown.

After the battle of the Alma I was ordered to take
my company on outlying picquet.   The night was
pitch dark, and my instructions were to communi-
cate with the 19th and 77th, the other two regiments of our brigade.   I could see nothing in
front, and in our rear were the bivouac fires of
the light division, and I heard no sound but the
murmur of the voices of the men.   At length I
was aware that some one mounted was approaching, and a voice said, 'Who is in command here?'
I advanced and explained my position.   The
owner of the voice gave me several instructions,
one of which was to light a fire, 'and, if anyone
asks you who gave you these orders, say General
Pennefather,' and he rode away.

The men of my picquet lit a fire, and very
soon after the picquets of the 19th and 77th
approached, attracted by the light, for they also
had been puzzled what to do.   We had not been
long settled when a clatter of cavalry sounded

coming towards us, and an English voice made the same observation the general had done! 'Who is in command here?' I made myself known, and great was my surprise to find Thompson of the 17th Lancers, with a detachment of his regiment, roaming about. For a moment or two we recalled old scenes in Paris; for he had formed one of that merry party. We shook hands, and he rode away. I never saw him again. He was killed in the charge of the light brigade at Balaclava.

Archdeacon Wright told a good story of a Connaught Ranger, after the battle of the Alma. When we moved on, and came to the river Katcha, where we halted for the night, there was near our bivouac a country house, which had been deserted by its inhabitants a very short time before our arrival. The property was a valuable one, and there were extensive cellars, in which were many large casks of wine. The archdeacon was roaming among them, when all of a sudden he came on a soldier of the Connaught Rangers, who, on being discovered, began to tap the big barrels with a stick, and appeared to listen attentively to the sound he made.

'What are you doing there, my friend?' said the archdeacon.

'May it plase yer riverence,' replied the man, 'I was looking for the well, and thought perhaps these barrels moight howld water.'

Some of the men of my company had also been looking for water, for they brought me a huge can full of the best red wine I ever tasted, and just in time; for an order was issued soon after forbidding the men to stray away from the lines of their regiments.

After the flank march through the woods—a most fatiguing performance—and having come to Mackenzie Farm, and the rear of Menschikoff's army, where his carriage was taken, in which was a drunken aide-de-camp, we continued on to Traktir Bridge, and next day advanced on Balaclava, which was easily captured. What a pretty smiling little harbour it was then! approached through vineyards laden with the most magnificent grapes.

I there received an order to remain in command of some men of the 88th, who were to form part of a dépôt under command of a colonel. The dépôt consisted of men from all the regiments. At first we bivouacked in the open, but, after a little, houses were appropriated for the men, and the officers had to shift for themselves. I found a cottage, in which was rather a pretty woman in great fear and distress. It was a clean little house, and I got some one to explain to the poor woman that her things would be safe, and that she might come and take them away whenever it suited her. So she seemed quite pleased, and presented me with some hens. I do not remember how she managed to get her things removed, but she and her property disappeared, and I was left in possession. A looking-glass, which now hangs on the wall in Monreith, is the only memento I have of that small house.

A very curious thing happened to me, which was very trying at the time, but in one way had its pleasing aspect, for it brought forth expressions of kindly feeling from men with whom I had small acquaintance. In the list of captains in the 88th I was fourth. George Vaughan Maxwell had been senior captain, but was promoted to be major. By some strange mistake, when the brevet came out in November or

December, 1854, my name appeared as brevet-major, although there were three captains senior to me. Colonel Shirley went to Lord Raglan, and brought to his lordship's notice the facts of the case: that my seniors were more entitled to the brevet than I was. Lord Raglan said it was a very hard case for my seniors, but that as I had received the brevet, the rule applied—once a major, always a major—and that I was a very lucky fellow.

So I did duty as a major, and commanded in the trenches as one—in short, was recognised as a brevet-major. But one cold winter's morn I was informed that my appointment was a mistake, and that I must return to my former rank as captain. It was a very trying position, but no fault of mine. Everyone sympathised with me, and, when I went on duty to the trenches, the officer in command, generally, to show how much he felt for me, gave me charge of some most exposed party, a kindness I would have most gladly dispensed with. My relations at home were very indignant—one sterling friend of mine was most energetic in her efforts to see me righted, and on one occasion attacked a great man in authority

G

so strongly that at length he rose, exclaiming,

'Duchess, I can remain no longer. I sit on a Board at two o'clock.'

'Well,' said her grace, 'I can only hope that it may be a *very hard one*.'

CHAPTER V.

THE PUNJAUB.

CHAPTER V.

DURING the siege of Sebastopol, the Connaught Rangers formed one of the left brigade, light division, the other regiments being the 19th and 77th. There was an officer belonging to the 19th who was a pure Scotchman. On being asked why he joined such a thoroughly English regiment as the 19th, he gave as his reason that his father was very old and his writing not distinct, and he had applied for his son to be appointed to the 79th Highlanders, but he had made the 7 so like a 1 that the authorities had gazetted him to the 19th.

When the final attack was made upon Sebastopol, the light division formed the storming party and supports. After running across the intervening ground between the trenches and the Redan, two hundred and eighty yards, and getting into the ditch and up on to the salient of the Redan, a check took place, and officers and men got no further. Some time elapsed, all the ammunition was expended, and no more was to be got. The Russians soon found this out, and charged us. The consequence was we were all sent tumbling over into the ditch which we had previously crossed. I fell flat among some poor fellows who never rose again, and my feelings of disgust were great when the above-mentioned officer put his foot—like a fiddle-case—in the centre of my back, and made use of me as a stepping-stone to get out of the ditch. I got out some way or other, and found myself, with many others, hurrying to our trenches, where I arrived in a very tattered condition. The first officer I met was my Scotch friend, who appeared greatly surprised to see me, and greeted me warmly, saying,

' Maxwell! is that you? I thought you were dead. Have a drink,' producing a flask, at which I was delighted to have a pull.

The siege was over, another winter had passed in luxury compared with the one that had gone before, summer was coming again, and the

Sebastopol heights were clothed with flowers, which hid both shot and shell beneath their green leaves. Peace was made, and we were all dreaming of home.

I was paying a visit to Sir Houston Stewart, in his flagship, the *Hannibal*, commanded by my old friend, Sir John Hay. We had a most pleasant party, among whom was Sir Henry Bernard, a genial and agreeable companion. He now lies in his grave in front of Delhi. A man-of-war, the *Belleisle*, was reported as having arrived, and it was decided that the 88th Regiment should return to England in her. I was ordered to telegraph to the regiment, and next day they embarked. We were all in the greatest spirits. I bid adieu to the kind admiral and all friends in the *Hannibal*, and proceeded on board the *Belleisle*. A fatigue party of the regiment was engaged at the capstan when a fearful accident happened. I cannot tell what the cause of it was, but I believe the man who watched the chain neglected his duty. I can only state, however, what occurred. All of a sudden the chain ran out with great velocity, round went the capstan, and out flew the bars like porcupine quills. I was standing on the poop, and one of the capstan bars hit me on the face and marked me for life; but, far worse, a soldier, named Burke, who had been all through the siege, was killed outright. Another man had his leg broken, and others were wounded severely. Sir Houston Stewart telegraphed home that the accident had occurred, and that I was all right. I am glad he did so, for my brother had received the telegram, before he read in a Scotch paper that I was killed.

As we sailed away from Kamiesch Bay the *Hannibal* manned the yards, and the officers and men of the Connaught Rangers loudly cheered farewell as we left the shores of the Crimea for ever. We were towed by H.M.S. *Firebrand*, commanded by a most agreeable officer, Captain the Honourable Spencer, whom it has never been my fortune to meet since those days.

The *Firebrand* remained with us till we arrived at the coast of Portugal, when she left us, owing to cholera being very bad on board her. We touched at Malta and Gibraltar, and anchored at the mouth of the Tagus. As cholera was raging at Lisbon, we were not allowed to land, but Captain Hoskins, our commander, asked me to accompany him in a sail in the cutter to Belem and Lisbon. We paid a visit to a man-of-war lying off the latter place, and met a young artillery officer on his way home from the Crimea. He was in great spirits, and had a dog he had brought with him from Sebastopol. He wanted me to land at Lisbon, and laughed a good deal when I informed him that we were not allowed to do so, owing to the prevalence of cholera. He said he had been often in the town, and was always quite well. We returned, however, to the *Belleisle* without landing.

Next morning, before putting to sea, Captain Hoskins received some letters from Lisbon, and startled us very much when he announced the death from cholera of that young officer we had met the day before. In process of time we arrived at Portsmouth. It was homelike to see once more the gay yachts skimming about between Cowes and Ryde; for it was the summer season. We landed, and were ordered to Aldershot, where we had the honour of parading before Her Majesty the Queen—two thousand strong. What a grand regiment might have been picked out of these splendid men! but most of them were discharged. The Indian Mutiny then broke out, but the best part of these warriors had been sent out of the service, and we bitterly felt their loss.

We came home in July, 1856, and in July, 1857, the Connaught Rangers embarked for India in course of relief.

When the 88th went out to India in 1857, as before mentioned, it was for the usual relief, and not in consequence of the mutiny; for, when we left the shores of Britain on the 9th of July, the terrible facts of the insurrection were unknown to us. I was in command of the left wing, which embarked at Portsmouth on board the good ship *Ulysses*, to proceed round the Cape to Calcutta. The *Ulysses* was a fine sailing vessel, chartered by Government to carry troops; her usual passengers being emigrants. The captain was a worthy Scotchman, but his ideas of comfort were limited. The morning we embarked, my brother having come to see me off, I asked him to breakfast on board. There was bread, and tea, and a bowl of boiled eggs, but no milk or butter. My brother took an egg and broke the shell, it was bad; he took another, it was worse; so he gave it up as a bad job, but the captain encouraged him to go on by saying, ' Crack awa, crack awa, ye'll soon come to a good yin.' I was obliged to make a report to the proper authorities, and the worthy man was enlightened as to the fact that officers of Her Majesty's regiments in those days were not to be treated like emigrants; and for the future we were fed in a cleaner and more wholesome manner. At Spithead we bade adieu to relations, friends, and acquaintances. And thirteen years passed away before I again looked upon the fair Isle of Wight and England's shores.

Our honest skipper, although quite unaccustomed to deal with gentlemen passengers, was a very kindly man. Evidently, in his former voyages, he had seen many a disagreeable quarrel among his emigrants, for he was very much afraid of any unpleasantness occurring. I proposed starting a newspaper, to be called the *Ulysses Gazette*, which was to come out every Saturday, in which anyone who pleased might write an article.

The old captain looked alarmed.

'Ye won't, colonel, have any pairsonaylities, I hope,' was his timid remark.

The *Gazette* came out, and was a great success. Some of my brother officers established a school on board, which was well attended by the men. We had a very good time, and all the officers were most friendly. I cannot say the same for the soldiers' wives (there were no ladies on board), who appealed to me sometimes as colonel on subjects regarding which my legal knowledge was not sufficient to instruct or help them.

When our ship came to a certain latitude we were surrounded day and night by Cape pigeons, graceful, white angels they looked in the pale moonlight, but most unpleasant birds when brought on board, as they immediately became vulgarly sick. Albatrosses soared above, and sharks followed us. When we were in the latitude of the Cape, the sea was the finest spectacle I ever saw. It ran mountains high, but it was as if oil had been poured on its surface. Our vessel rose up to the summit of one of those unbroken hills, and then glided down the other side, just to rise up again. It was a wonderful sight.

In the month of November we anchored off the Sandheads, having left England on the 9th of July, and never having sighted land the whole way till we saw the shores of India. We now received the astounding intelligence of all the horrors of the mutiny, and the perplexing news that Delhi was taken. Taken by whom? We had been so long at sea we knew nothing. In a day or two we landed at Calcutta, and our gallant ship, which had brought us safely out, was wrecked on her way home. Fortunately, however, the captain and crew were saved.

When the Connaught Rangers first landed at Calcutta the great shock of the mutiny was being severely felt. Very few of us knew anything about the ways of the country, and we were, so to speak, cast adrift in a foreign land. We had great difficulty in procuring anything. I shall not enlarge on these troubled times. The generation that lived through them is passing away, and with them is fading the intense bitterness that the fearful atrocities of Cawnpore called forth—so utterly forgotten now that I read books that make high-minded remarks on the unforgiving spirit that actuated us in those days. It is better to forget; but the retribution was not too heavy for the crimes committed.

In this country good or bad servants seem a very minor consideration; not so in India, where comfort is so essentially in the hands of domestics. One of our greatest difficulties in landing was procuring any. All the good servants had vanished, and for some time we were obliged to be satisfied with a very inferior lot. One of my brother officers got a man called Paul, a miserable little man, who was always getting drunk. When we marched to Cawnpore after the capture of Calpee, a great many men of the regiment got fever, and, among other officers, Paul's master was very ill. The wretched servant got drunk in the bazaar, and was made a prisoner—at least, so it was supposed, for he did not return to his master, and no one knew what had become of him. Time went on and my brother officer got better, and *pour passer le temps* either rode or drove into the town of Cawnpore to look at the place still stained with the blood of its victims. Either by chance or from a desire to see the sepoy prisoners, my friend arrived at the kotwallee or guard-house where these mutineers were incarcerated, and, to his great dismay, he saw among these ironed rebels a wretched little man, who shouted: 'Me Paul! me poor Paul!' Much surprised, he went to the kotwal and asked why the man was among the rebels, but could get no satisfactory reply. On explaining matters that most probably Paul had been locked up for drunkenness, and not rebellion, he got him released, as one of the policemen grimly observed, 'just in time, for he would have been hanged in to-morrow's batch.'

Paul left Cawnpore without much delay.

The story of the mutiny has been told over and over again. In time it was stamped out, but for a long period distant murmurings were still heard like those of a thunder-storm fading away. Gradually the air cleared, and Marochetti's 'Angel of Peace' was placed on the Cawnpore Well. Beautiful flowers began to grow in a garden where once women and children were dragged to their death, and writers at home began to publish books to prove that all the horrors, murders, and atrocities were caused by the fault of the white inhabitants of India. So I pass over that sad and nearly forgotten time, and, leaping over several years, come to the year 1866, when the 88th Connaught Rangers proceeded to the Punjaub.

In the autumn of 1866 the Connaught Rangers, which I had then the honour to command, was ordered to proceed from Cawnpore, where we had been stationed for some time, to Rawul Pindee in the Punjaub. We were directed to halt, on our way up country, at Agra, to form part of a large camp there, to be assembled for the grand durbar to be held in honour of the installation of the Star of India. All the rajahs, princes, and begums of the empire were to be present, to meet Lord Lawrence, governor-general.

On our arrival at Agra, we found a very large force collected. We were nearly all under canvas, and so also were the princes of India, with their numerous retinues. The governor-general came into Agra the day after our arrival there, and from that hour the cannons of the fort and batteries had a hard time of it. As every prince went to wait on the viceroy a salute was fired, and, according to the number of rounds fired, we inferred the rank of the great man who sallied forth to cross the plain, followed by his marvellous suite of elephants, carrying gorgeously mounted howdahs, warriors riding on prancing pink-nosed horses, with tails and legs deeply dyed with red, to represent the blood of their enemies, down to the tag-rag and bobtail that are inseparable from the courts of those native princes.

The durbar was a magnificent sight. There we saw gathered together most of the great powers of India; the Begum of Bhopaul, our steady friend, men that had done us good service during our evil times, and others who had done us as little as they could. All had been rewarded, as far as possible, according to their works. Each noble vied with his neighbour in the number and beauty of his ornaments, and the rays of the sun blazed on priceless jewels.

But our stay at Agra was not a period of idleness. Reviews and sham battles kept the troops occupied from hour to hour. I had command of a brigade, and often left my tent before the dawn, when night still darkened all around, and the stars alone lit up the sky. It was during the month of November, and the fall of meteors was constantly to be seen; their appearance as they

H

fell in dazzling brightness being most startling and sublime. From all parts of the compass they came. First a long stream of light, which reminded me of the 'bouquets' the Russians sent us during the siege of Sebastopol, and then a ball of fire, which burst like a rocket, leaving all in darkness again. And so it continued till the sun rose in its splendour, and the air became full of noisy life.

As a variety to our military morning work, there were various large dinners, given by the governor-general and the commander-in-chief. There were dances also. The Rajah of Jeypore entertained us all at a splendid ball, and Scindia illuminated the Taj. We should have enjoyed our halt at Agra very much had not that dreadful curse, cholera, invaded the camp, and caused the loss of several valuable lives. One night my wife alarmed me by assuring me that she felt very ill. The medicine-chest was in our other large tent, where my wife's maid slept, at some distance from the one we were occupying. I got hold of my bearer, and, writing a note, dispatched him with it to M'Kay, the maid. After some

delay, she appeared, very lightly clad, with my
note in her hand, saying, 'A man had come a
long way with this, and wanted the colonel to get
it at once.' Her knowledge of Hindostani was
limited, and she had not recognised the bearer.

CHAPTER VI.

DELHI.

CHAPTER VI.

OWING to the fell presence of the grim
visitor, cholera, the durbar broke up
sooner than was intended, and my regiment received orders to proceed by train to Delhi, *en
route* to Rawul Pindee. My wife not being very
well, I decided to go on at night by passenger
train. The left wing of the regiment was to
follow by special train, but the station-master was
not certain when he could despatch them, leaving
a wide margin, between 6 p.m. or 1 a.m. 3 a.m.
saw us, tired and miserable, at our journey's
end, standing on the railway platform, without
a coolie to help us with our luggage, or any more
light than the glimmer our own lantern afforded.
Such was the Delhi railway-station in 1866.

A gharry was at last procured, and wearied
and worn we started for the hotel (which had

been our mess-house when the Rangers were stationed here in 1859). The railway did not cross the river Jumna, which was spanned by a bridge of boats. This entailed further delay, as the pair of ponies had to be taken out and changed for bullocks before we ventured on the swaying structure. But the longest and most tedious journey ends at last, and so did ours as we stopped at Hamilton's hotel. It was bitterly cold, and as in India the traveller carries his own bedding, and our luggage was still at the station, we had not a very comfortable night's rest. As the morning advanced everything looked brighter. The weather was perfect, reminding one of a breezy autumn day at home. We drove out to the camp, which we found pitched in the old cantonments outside Delhi, where our army was encamped so long during the memorable siege in 1857.

As we left Delhi we passed through the Cashmere Gate, a monument now of gallant daring. My tents were pitched under a tope of trees, and the breeze sighing among the branches sounded like the wind up aloft at sea. We met a great many regiments at Delhi, as it was the relief season, and they were all on their way to new quarters. It made the difficulty greater than usual of getting carriage conveyance.

Being delayed several days, we spent our time visiting the sights in and near Delhi, specially the palace in whose vast hall, with its many pillars of marble, once stood the peacock throne, which was carried away by Nadir Shah in 1739. Along the cornice on each side of the chamber there is written in Arabic the inscription, ' If there be a paradise on earth, it is this, it is this, it is this!' The dilapidated state the whole of the palace was in when I first saw it in 1859 might have saddened anyone, but on this last visit what a change! Everything had been cared for, and the poetical beauty of the place was brought out with great success. In Delhi stands the Jumna-Musjid, *i.c.*, the Friday mosque, Friday being the Mohammedan Sabbath. At the siege in 1857 our soldiers forced their way into this temple. A very great friend of mine, Coghill, who was then adjutant of the 2nd Fusiliers, was cheering the men on in his gallant, hearty way, and he came to what was called the holy of holies, a structure made in imitation of the prophet's tomb at Mecca. Coghill seized hold of the koran, a large and heavy book kept in this place, and carried it off with several other wonders, such as a hair of the prophet's moustache, and similar trustworthy valuables. As the koran was rather heavy, he handed it over to some one to take to one of the civilian officers.

After Delhi had fallen, I was anxious to get a remembrance of the great siege, and I became possessor of the koran. For a long time it reposed in one of my portmanteaus, but a native came to see me one day and said that it was known by certain Mohammedans that a copy of the koran was in my possession, and that it was very valuable, being one of the three original copies, one of which was at Mecca, another at Delhi, and the last I forget where. So I packed it up very carefully and sent it home to Scotland. Thinking that the Bodleian library would value such an acquisition, I offered it through a friend, but was informed that the koran was incomplete; so it still belongs to me.

Among many interesting accounts of Delhi, there is none more curious than that contained in the autobiography of Sultan Baber, who lived

A.D. 1526. He was the ancestor of the old king of Delhi, who lost his throne by the mutiny of 1857. Baber was born to the throne of Ferghana, or Transosian, now the Russian province of Khokan. Sherbany Khan, the leader of the Usbegs, took all from him, but Baber (which means tiger) conquered all his overwhelming difficulties by his energy and courage. He gained the throne of Kabul, and was ruler of that country in A.D. 1525. As he had many adherents, he determined to invade India. Sultan Baber wrote his own autobiography in a dialect of the Turkish language; it was translated into Persian, and also into English fifty years ago by Dr. Leyden. The civilization of India is Turkish to this day. Until the year 1857 Baber's descendants continued to reign in Delhi. 'There are four roads,' writes Baber, 'that lead from Kabul to India; in all these there are passes more or less difficult, Lamghanat and Kheiber, Bangash, Naghz, and Fernul.' The Lamghanat road is the present route from Kabul to Peshawur, and it was by it that Baber and his horsemen marched, and his baggage and cannon were conveyed; it was the scene of the Kabul massacre in 1842, when a

British army was cut to pieces; it witnessed the triumphal march of a British army in 1879.

'A.D. 1526, April 12th—The Turks, under Baber, arrived within two marches of Panipat— which lies fifty miles from Delhi—and on the 21st of April the battle was fought that gave India foreign masters for many centuries, and a form of government that it still retains.'

'The same night, April 21st, A.D. 1526, Prince Humayon and Kurajeh Khan were despatched to take Agra, seventy miles away. Baber marched to Delhi. Delhi for three thousand years had been a great city. It was contemporaneous with Nineveh and Babylon. The city of Delhi of that day was called Firozabad. On a rocky hill, which extends on one side of the city, was a citadel, built by King Feroze a hundred years before the Turkish invasion. On another side of the city was King Feroze's other palace, in which stood a trophy of war, a large monolith of stone, surmounted by the Moslem emblem of the crescent shining in brass. On it were inscriptions in the Pali tongue, which recalled a long-forgotten king, Asoka, the King Alfred of Hindoo history.'

All this information I copied at the time of reading it—the most interesting account of Sultan Baber's journal. When I was quartered in Delhi, in 1859, I have often ridden over to these ancient ruins, and examined the inscriptions on the stone pillar, which had then lost the Moslem emblem mentioned above. The courtyard was then used for the commissariat bullocks, and the dust, flying about everywhere, was almost blinding. Delhi, in ancient times, was the largest city in Hindostan, covering a space of twenty square miles. It has now dwindled down to a circumference of seven miles; but the ruins of its former grandeur still exist, and a vast tract is covered with remains of palaces and mausoleums. We drove out to the Kootub-minar, that wonderful monument of a by-gone age. We passed on our way the once famous observatory, now much dilapidated, and no longer used for astronomical observation. In the eleven miles' drive we saw a succession of tombs, generally solid, square edifices, with domed tops. We stopped at the mausoleum of Sufter Jung, which stands in a garden, and is a graceful reminiscence of a prince of Oude. After a dusty drive across a sandy plain, we thought the patch of green on which the Kootub stands, with its shady trees, a most refreshing sight.

Passing through Aladdin's Gate, a very fine arch, we saw before us the splendid column of the 'Minar.' It rises in a succession of marvellous sculptured fluted columns, two hundred and forty feet high, very wide at the base, and diminishing in circumference at each series of joints till the summit is reached. Like the campaniles attached to churches abroad, whence the bells ring out their summons to prayer, so from the height of the Kootub the faithful were called to their devotions in the adjacent mosque. Sultan Baber, in his journal, mentions the Kootub as 'that strange, tall, unrivalled pillar, which was raised to call the faithful to prayer in the splendid mosque open to the blue heavens below.' We were informed that the Kootub had been erected by a prince, to enable his daughter to ascend every day and look upon the holy river Jumna, a feat which, if performed by her, must have kept her in first-rate condition, for the Kootub is, I think, higher than the Monument of London, and the winding stair is very steep.

At length we were enabled to leave Delhi. There is no more agreeable duty than a long march in India during the cold weather. After all the necessary preparations have been made; after the means of transport have been collected, and various other arrangements, trying to the temper and patience of commanding-officer, adjutant, and quarter-master, have been got over, the regimental order-book contains the following announcement, that 'The regiment will parade at 3 a.m.,' the next day. On the same evening that these orders are read to the companies, a detachment has marched away, with the camp color-men and the married people; the former to lay out the lines of the camp, the latter to be out of the way of the regiment.

I always sent on a tent to be pitched by my own native servants, and, when we arrived at the camping ground in the morning, we found everything ready. What luxurious tents these were! Each one consisted of a drawing-room, bed-room, and dressing-room, with a broad verandah, formed by an outer covering. Indian servants have a wonderful knack of arranging a room. As the tent we slept in was denuded of all furniture, excepting beds and a chair or two, when we arrived in the morning, we entered apparently the same sitting-room we had occupied the previous day. Not a book was in a different place—everything was the same. On some marches we rode in advance of the regiment, on others we drove in my wife's carriage ; but, whichever way we travelled, we enjoyed ourselves much. The Grand Trunk road of India, along which we were journeying, was the finest made road in the world, smooth, and level as a billiard-table. Ten to twelve miles was the average length of a day's march.

The men throve wonderfully. It was splendid to see them quickening their swinging steps as they came in sight of the new camping ground, marching in, every man in his ranks, to the lively sound of the band, playing 'Patrick's Day in the Morning.' As each company came to its camping ground, it was halted, and piled arms by command of its captain, and then the men proceeded to pitch the tents. It was a fine sight to behold. When the bugle sounded a long, melancholy note, as if by magic a white canvas town rose up on the dusty plain.

Then a sudden lull would fall on the busy scene. The men were preparing for breakfast. The camels, eased of their loads, were driven off to find their food in the neighbourhood; the patient bullocks lay by their carts, and munched chopped straw, or ruminated on the hardships of their life, while the married women of the regiment, having arrived the night before, were the only visible people, and they were occupied scolding their servants; for in India all Europeans are waited on, and the wives of privates have their cooks and their washermen. The married soldiers' families on a long march travelled in large bamboo cages, covered with carpeting to keep out the sun as much as possible, and these cages were put on the common country carts, drawn by bullocks. We had a long line of fifty or sixty carts of married people, and, as they started in advance at about two in the afternoon on the same day as the regiment marched in, a great hush always seemed to fall on the camp as they creaked and groaned off on their way. The fresh early morning is very exhilarating, and the days are never too hot in the cold weather.

I

One morning was very cold, so my wife and I rode quickly on in front of the battalion. We passed the camels, which were moving steadily along on each side of the well-made Indian highway. We arrived too soon at the camping ground, and our tents were not quite ready, as the servants had not expected us so early; so we got chairs, and sat enjoying the fresh morning air. At length our camels, told off to carry the khansama's property, arrived. On one of these 'ships of the desert' was fastened a hencoop containing some turkeys and fowls. My wife insisted that the poultry should be released at once, which was done, and a huge white turkey rushed madly about, and finally jumped on to my wife's lap. She received the great bird with kindness, but in a short time exclaimed, in accents of the greatest consternation:—'Oh, Edward, the turkey has laid an egg in my lap!' And so it had. How we laughed! That turkey was ever after a great pet, was named Lady Alicia, and travelled with us for many a day, but at length was devoured by a jackal in the hills of Murree.

At Kurnal we found our tents pitched in a

pretty spot, under large trees, just outside the walls of the town. But we were carried off by an old friend, Colonel Trench, superintendent of the government stud at Kurnal, to his bungalow. Tent life is very pleasant, but after a long time of it one appreciates the solid comforts of four walls and a roof. The stud was a very interesting sight, everything being in the most perfect order. There were about eight hundred horses altogether, three hundred of them colts. We saw them turned out for exercise in a large field. How they tore about, with manes and tails streaming! Then they formed up, with distended nostrils, to have a look at us, and were off again. Kurnal used to be one of the largest and most favourite stations in India; but it became, from some unknown reason, dreadfully unhealthy. Hundreds of Europeans died there, and it was abandoned as a military station.

We spent Christmas here. Christmas is a season of rejoicing in India to the natives as well as to us. Yellow flowers are profusely used as decorations, and it is the custom for all the principal employés to present 'dollies' to their masters, or the heads of departments. As colonel commanding a regiment, I received 'dollies' from the kotwal of the regimental bazaar, from the commissariat baker, and many others, and now on the march the chief of the camel-men brought a hill 'dollie.' They are almost always of the same shape, that of a large, round, flat basket, with the contents tastefully arranged so that everything is seen at once. Oranges, pomegranates, raisins, sugar, spices, and Cabul grapes, packed up in little boxes, each grape in cotton wool, are the usual gifts. To touch the basket with the right hand, in sign of acceptance, is sufficient, and then the servants get the contents, or, if there is any special delicacy, you appropriate it.

Umballa, a very large station, was our next important halt. Its close vicinity to the hills and Simla makes it very popular. The band of the 94th Regiment came out to meet the 88th. None of us thought then that in a few years that gallant corps would be called the 2nd Battalion Connaught Rangers. We changed our carts and camels at Umballa, and were delayed fifteen days before we got others. We met with the greatest hospitality and kindness, and our time passed pleasantly. One night we were fairly washed out of our tents by a most tremendous storm which suddenly burst over us. The thunder roared, the lightning flashed incessantly, and the heavens descended in a flood. Our tents were ankle deep in water. Daylight showed that the camp was standing in a lake. The men, who on a march have no beds, were badly off; but the greatest sufferers were the married women and children. Their cages had been necessarily removed from the carts that had conveyed them from Delhi, and they were on the ground till we got our new supply of carriages. Poor women, every stitch they possessed was floating in water. The sun, fortunately, came out, and tents and clothes dried; but we moved to another ground.

About three hundred miles from Delhi we halted at Umritsur, celebrated for its golden temple; the walls are of pure white marble, and its roof of copper gilt. It stands in a miniature lake, a hundred and fifty paces square, the water of which, when we were there, was green and stagnant, and in it the Sikhs immerse themselves, that they may be purified from their sins. I think that the Temple of Umritsur looks more imposing in a photograph than in reality. We passed along the marble causeway, guarded on each side with golden balustrades and lamps, and paused at the solid silver door to have straw shoes put over our boots. The inside is richly gilded and decorated, and the marble floor is inlaid with mosaic; but there is a tawdriness in the silken canopy, under which reposes the sacred 'Grunth,' the Sikh's Bible, and in the yellow flowers hung everywhere.

Umritsur has always been noted for its manufacture of shawls and silks, and owing to its situation between Cabul, Delhi, and Cashmere, has driven a great trade.

There was intense excitement one night in consequence of a robber having been caught close to our tent, stark naked, and greased from head to foot. The servants surrounded him, but could not hold him till the bheestee (water-carrier) poured a mussock of water over him and he was rubbed down. There is a regular caste of thieves. The mess one night lost all their copper pots and pans.

On the 23rd of February, 1867, we marched into Rawul Pindee, after a journey which was most successfully accomplished. We were quite sorry the long march was over. The men were in most splendid condition. The usual amount of difficulty in collecting transport going up country had been encountered, but everything had gone right at last. We all had had pleasant meetings with old friends at the various stations we had passed. At several of them my wife and I had stopped for a night or two at a friend's bungalow, driving on afterwards, and overtaking the regiment, which had always been moving steadily on. So it was with real regret we watched the departure from camp on the last day's march. The four bullock-carts started with the servants, the goats dragging behind. The wives of the chief men were in marching trim, with tight blue trousers down to their heavily-bangled ankles, and over their heads was a great white square of linen, reaching to their waists; behind them again was the swaying line of camels.

The Rangers had owned a pack of fox-hounds, which had given many a good day's run in the plains of the North West, and it was to our great dismay we were told, on being ordered to Rawul Pindee, that our pack would be of no use up there. So they were disposed of before we left

Cawnpore, and when we saw the broken country we had got into, we felt we had done wisely to sell them. The hot weather was very near when we reached Pindee. We had just time to get comfortably housed and settled when it was upon us.

CHAPTER VII.

THE AMEER OF CABUL.

CHAPTER VII.

RAWUL PINDEE is one of the most favourite quarters, being so close to the hill station of Murree. Four hours carries one from the breathless heat of the plain to the top of a mountain, with an elevation of seven thousand four hundred and fifty-seven feet.

My wife and I were eager to make an expedition during the leave season into Cashmere. The mountains guarding the Happy Valley had stood out, a grand rampart, clear on the horizon, a great part of our march. Our plans were all arranged. Light tents were bought, and leave was obtained, when cholera made its appearance in the regiment. Of course going away then was out of the question. The married people were sent—to their great discomfort—into camp, and extraordinary precautions were taken to prevent the spread of the disease, the horrors of which we had so lately seen.

When encamped at Agra, under the outer flap of my tent, two unfortunate natives lay down and died during the night, only the canvas walls between them and us. Mercifully, the present outbreak was a slight one. But, when we could get away, there was not time left, during the leave season, for our journey to Cashmere, so we contented ourselves with a visit to Murree, the sanitorium of this district.

No one who has not experienced real hot weather in the plains, can understand what Indian heat is. It means darkness, for one thing, as every ray of light is carefully excluded. In our darkened house at Pindee, with every precaution taken, for a fortnight the thermometer never varied, night and day, from 99°. But, oh, the joy of the first rain! When doors and windows were thrown open, and we once again saw each other!

Rawul Pindee was a very hospitable place. I remember dining with one of the civilians. It was a very grand party. Everything went off charmingly. The soup was hot, the champagne well iced, and the inevitable tinned salmon, with Tartare sauce, was in abundance. As I observed that those who took salad tasted it, and left it alone, I took none. Next day my wife called on our hostess, and found her nearly in tears.

' Oh, Mrs. Maxwell,' she exclaimed, in horrified accents, ' can you believe it? The khansama made the salad with castor oil !'

We were quartered a year at Rawul Pindee, and then received orders to march to Peshawur.

We remained twelve months at Peshawur, and although there was a good deal of fever, yet we did not suffer so much as the 42nd Royal High-landers, whom we relieved, had done. During the time they were quartered there that un-fortunate regiment was decimated by cholera and fever. Not only did they lose many men, but their pipers nearly all succumbed.

The most noteable event which occurred when we were at that station was the visit of the Ameer of Cabul, on his way to Umballa to meet Lord Mayo. The whole division paraded to do him honour, and, as I commanded a brigade, I had a good view of this treacherous man. Certainly his appearance was very noble and soldier-like. He rode with the general and staff in front of our line, mounted on a high-bred Turcoman mare. I was so taken up looking at this perfect animal, that I had no eyes for the rider; but I saw him often afterwards, and my remembrance of Shere Ali is not that of an artful deceiver, but more of a frank, jolly soldier. But at that time he was full of hope that our government would stand by him, and his heart must have beat with pleasure when he looked on the bronzed warriors of Britain as they were in those days. Besides, he must have felt elated when he saw not only the chivalry of India assembled to do him honour, but all the civilians, men and women, crowding to get a sight of him.

My wife rode to the parade, but when she got to the ground the crowd was so great that she dismounted from her nag and got into the howdah on the back of an elephant, which sapient animal knelt down to allow her to ascend the ladder, the only way to get up. As she had begun the morning on horseback, she was dressed in a riding-habit, and had on her head a tall hat. When the parade was over, and the regiments were still formed up, Shere Ali rode away, and, passing the elephant on which my wife was seated, seemed rather perplexed at her dress, and evidently asked for an explanation. But before the Ameer returned to his country he saw many things more astonishing than a lady in a riding-habit.

During our stay at Peshawur, Bishop Milman, who was beloved by everyone, visited the station. The greatest regret was expressed when very soon after his visit to us he was drowned, having fallen into the river when going up a slippery plank which had been placed to enable him to go on board a steamer. My remembrance of this good man is, that he was very stout, had a deep voice, and preached a most impressive sermon on the text 'Redeem the time.'

I mention all this to show how utterly absurd was the statement made about him by a fraudulent mess-man. A regiment quartered near us invited the bishop to dinner, an invitation which he accepted. It appears that the mess sergeant had been for some time suspected of not being very honest in his charges, and he was watched by one of the mess committee. The day after the bishop had dined at the mess the accounts were over-hauled, and the enormous number of twenty glasses of brandy and soda were charged against the mess guests.

'This is impossible,' said the officer making the inquiry, 'the number is too great.'

'Not at all, sir,' said the mess sergeant, 'the bishop alone had fourteen tumblers!'

We passed a very pleasant time at Peshawur, and regretted when the order came for us to move to Nowshera. Peshawur is situated on the River Bara, and is twelve miles from the Khyber Pass. The cantonments are on a ridge at a higher elevation than the town, which is very unhealthy. Cholera and fever commit great havoc there, and yet it is a fair place to look upon, with its gardens and green trees, and curiously-shaped bungalows built of mud, as earthquakes are very common during the cold weather, and the houses formed of mud consolidated in a wooden frame are less dangerous than stone-built edifices.

Peshawur cantonments suffer not only from fever, but from the occasional inroads of robbers, who are very clever at their trade, and steal horses in a wonderful manner. To save himself from their attacks, a kind of black-mail is paid by every person who is head of a house, and who desires security. This monthly tax is given to men called 'chokedars,' and the recipients of the money belong to the hill tribes that guard the Khyber Pass; magnificent men and true as steel—so long as you pay them. They dress in a most picturesque costume, and are armed with several weapons, one of which is generally a blunderbuss. They march round your house all night, shouting at intervals, 'Khubardar!' (take care), a signal to their brother robbers that the sahib round whose house they are watching has paid the black-mail. The man in my service, a very handsome fellow, was always at his post; and I admired my brigand very much. One day he asked for leave, and, after bringing a friend of his to take his duty in his absence, he entered into a long story to my bearer, who, when I asked him why my chokedar wished leave, gave me the information desired in the following few words: 'Your highness,' said the bearer, with his hands clasped, 'this man wishes to go and murder his mother.' Of course, on learning that he was going on such a praiseworthy errand, I gave him his *congé*, and I never saw him again.

We were much commiserated when our turn for being quartered at Nowshera came round; but somehow we got on very well. Polo became a great institution, and we fraternised well with the cavalry and native regiments we found there. The Guides, at Murdan, a march across the river from Nowshera, always made any of us who visited them more than welcome. So, what with excursions to Peshawur, and occasional visits of friends passing up and down the Grand Trunk road, time passed pleasantly enough.

Nowshera is one of the hottest stations in the Punjaub—surrounded as it is by sandy hills —and when we first went to it there were no trees. Many hundreds were planted under my rule, and I am always gratified to hear that there is quite an avenue now from the barracks to the church. Camels are the great enemies of trees. Carefully as the young growth may be guarded, a long neck suddenly protrudes from the line of moving animals, and the top of a tree is nipped off, and its future beauty spoiled. But camels are not the only enemies trees may have; for, at my old home at Monreith, in Scotland, when this century was young, my father was possessed of many race-horses, one of which won the Leger. The stables are at some distance from the house, and my grandfather had planted several trees, which have grown up with forked tops. This unfortunate disfigurement was caused by the jockeys, on their way to the stables, flicking off the tops of the young trees with their riding whips; at least, so the old people at home say.

Nowshera is forty miles from Peshawur. When we were there, in 1868, there was nothing to be seen but a large barracks like a prison situated on the right of the Trunk Road from Peshawur to Attock. When the leave season came round, there was no cholera to prevent me getting away, so I decided to apply for six months' leave, and to spend them in Cashmere. Our tents, three in number, were as light as they could possibly be made. I took the precaution to have one of them thoroughly waterproof, as a refuge in very bad weather, but it proved unnecessary, as even in the trial of long continued rain none of the other tents leaked.

The horses and *impedimenta* preceded us by

a few days from Nowshera, and we were to over-take them at Rawul Pindee. My wife's steed, called by her 'Nila,' was a gentle, well-bred, grey Cabul, full of spirit when required. The way it came into my possession was rather curious. During the time we were at Peshawur, the late General Haly was in command, and, among many other good qualities, he knew a horse right well.

I have sometimes accompanied him into the town of Peshawur, where there were several horse-dealers. It was a risky thing going along the narrow streets of that town, filled as they were with wild-looking Afghans and Affrie-dees armed to the teeth; but we never were insulted. A dealer told General Haly that he had a horse, and invited him to see it. This visit ended in my buying the nag for a very small sum.

Next day the dealer came to my bungalow accompanied by a young Afghan, who was leading the horse. This young man placed the rope holding the steed in my hand. He put his arms round the animal's neck, kissed it on the fore-head, burst into tears, and then disappeared. Of course we asked an explanation of this scene,

and were informed by the dealer that the young
Afghan had come to Peshawur and lost all his
money (most probably to the dealer). He had nothing left but his horse, and so he sold it, 'and your
royal highness has got a bargain,' said the dealer,
finishing his story, a conclusion which meant a
demand for backsheesh. And Nila was a right
good nag. My pony, called Silver Tail, was the
most active, savage little brute I ever saw. He
could walk very fast, and scrambled over rocks in
a wonderful manner.

I cannot start on our Cashmere journey, during
which we met with some adventures, without
mentioning my wife's maid, M'Kay. She was
born in the Highlands, and a more devoted,
warm-hearted woman never lived. She rests in
her grave at Nowshera, but she is most kindly
remembered by both my wife and myself, for
whose comforts she made many sacrifices. It
was on a fine evening in April, when the fiery
sun was dipping behind the wall of mountains
that guard, what alas! has been too well named,
the 'Valley of Death,' that we left Nowshera in a
dāk carriage. The usual difficulty of getting the
horses to start was at length overcome, and, with

the accompaniment of whips cracking and men shouting, the little nags dashed off at a gallop, which they kept up for nearly the whole stage of seven miles. Fresh, wild-looking steeds were then harnessed, and we started again, with the same cracking of whips and shouting, the frightened animals tearing along over the beautifully-made Trunk Road.

Thus we hastened until we arrived at the banks of the mighty Indus. The river was tearing down in full summer flood. The bridge of boats, which was the usual means of crossing, had been removed, as was always done at this season. Our only way to transport ourselves and effects over, was by boats. We left the gharry here, and had to embark in an enormous barge. What a wild scene it was! The moon shone brightly on the troubled waters of the sacred river, which rushed along in frightful rapidity. The naked boatmen, armed with huge poles instead of oars, appeared like the forms we see in a feverish dream. When we were seated in this boat, which we could imagine to be Charon's, the word was shouted, and, by a vigorous push, we were sent out into the wild rush of waters. The black figures strained every nerve to keep our craft's head straight for the opposite shore, but the stream whirled us down the dark river which surged around us. Our crew made a tremendous effort, and we felt ourselves swept out of the main current into comparatively smooth waters, while the foaming river hurried along in furious haste. Then came the slow and arduous process of rowing up against the strong current to the place of disembarkation at Attock. Here we found two other gharries awaiting us, and, without further adventures, we went on the remainder of our way. The sun was rising when we trotted into Rawul Pindee. We halted at Roberry's Hotel during the heat of the day, and in the evening drove out to Barracao, a dāk bungalow at the foot of the hills, where we found our advance guard of servants and horses awaiting us.

Very early the next morning we may say we began our march to Cashmere. My wife was mounted on Nila. M'Kay was conveyed in a dandy, a kind of a sack fastened to a pole and carried by two coolies. I was on Silver Tail, and, the word being given, off we started, our four dogs, full of glee, racing before us. Quite dark when we left Barracao, the sun had risen by the time we got among the hills, but his light did not reveal much beauty of scenery. We were shut in almost the whole way by hills, covered for the most part with scrubby underwood, here and there diversified by patches of cultivation.

A constant stream of natives, donkeys, and mules seemed to be going up and down the mountain. Occasionally we passed a cart heavily laden with furniture and boxes plodding its weary way, at the rate of little more than a mile an hour, to where the anxious owners of its contents had been most probably expecting its arrival for many days. Sometimes minus a wheel, it reclines by the wayside, the servants in charge sitting calmly round the wreck, smoking the pipe of contentment. The four unyoked bullocks chew the cud, little caring how long matters progress —or rather do not progress—in the same way.

We enjoyed the morning ride very much. There was an elastic feeling in the air that re-called to our memory the Highlands of Scotland when the sun shone brightly in our far-away home, and our own glorious mountains towered around, clothed in their brilliant haze of purple heather. That night we halted at ' Tret,' and the next morning rode into Murree.

Murree was in 1868 a pretty, green-wooded place, but it lacked the grandeur of the other hill stations we had visited. Its precipices are banks, its mountains hills, compared with those of Simla or Mussoorie. It has no snowy range, like that grand chain of mountains one sees from the heights of Landour.

We passed some very pleasant days at Murree with Colonel (now Sir Samuel) Browne, G.C.B. His pretty two-storied house was situated on the side of a hill, which could only be reached by a very break-neck path. We were warmly welcomed by our kind and charming hostess, and enjoyed our visit very much. Murree is the starting-point for Cashmere, and the hiring of coolies to carry the baggage, &c., &c., is all completed here, for everything must be carried by men. After a most arduous undertaking, we succeeded at length in making our final arrangements, and, having said farewell to our kind hosts, we got on our horses and started for Cashmere.

All our baggage was carried by coolies. Those in British territory were a grumbling lot, who never were satisfied, and ran away very often, when they had been paid, as the civil authorities in those days insisted that the coolies should receive their small fee before starting on the journey.

We rode along the wooded road that leads from Murree, breathing the balmy afternoon breeze, which was laden with the sweet perfume of the pine forest. How glorious it was to feel free from all troubles, and to leave behind us all annoyances! . . . . What is this we see before us, left in the solemn woods? Our bedding, deserted by the coolie whose duty it was to carry it, and who had absconded altogether. I shouted, but only echo answered. The evening was closing fast, and nothing could be done. All along the line of march various articles belonging to us were left nestling among the mountain flowers, so we gave up attempting to collect our baggage, as some of our servants formed a rear-guard, and we pushed on to Deywal.

Deywal is a good-sized village, situated on the right side of a deep gorge, traversed by a stream, which flows into the Jhellum some miles down the mountain. There is now a good dāk bungalow near the village, but in 1868 there was only a rest-house. A couple of chairs, a table, and a charpoy (the bedstead of India), formed the furniture of this inhospitable dwelling, as in India travellers provide all their own necessaries of life, and our comforts were resting on the line of march, so we had to make the best of it; but our cook, having preceded us, we got some dinner. We had to repose our wearied limbs without any mattress, sheets, or pillows. My wife gallantly placed her head on her leather hand-bag, and declared she was 'very comfortable.' I used the privilege of a British soldier, and grumbled to my heart's content.

Previous to retiring for the night, we sat outside, enjoying the cool evening air. Immediately in front of us was the deep valley dividing us from high mountains on the other side. Light sparkled on this dark and lowering curtain from villages scattered over the distant view. High up on these fir-clad hills we could only guess, by the aid of the soft light of the moon, where our soldiers, who were occupied in making a princely road from Murree to Abbottabad, were encamped. The whole scene was grand to a degree, and as we adjourned for the night we cast our longing eyes towards the Cashmere hills, whose everlasting snow seemed ghost-like in the moon's white beams.

In the morning a miserable, forlorn-looking object arrived with a lantern in his hand. This poor wretch sat down and wept! To my dismay, I recognised my bearer. This draggled-looking object was generally a most consequential little man—of very high caste, and so honest that he could be trusted with any amount of money, and not a farthing would be purloined by him. My two bullock-trunks and a lantern he considered his special charge, and often afterwards, high up in the mountains of Cashmere, this little man might have been seen, with the lantern in one hand, and laden with his copper cooking-pots, which no one was of high enough caste to carry except himself. He had passed a night of misery; in dread that the thieves would rob the 'Sahib's' things. He was also in deadly fear that bears would demolish himself, and in terror lest evil spirits of the mountains might carry him away to some far off Gehenna;

and—what in reality was the greatest trial of all —he was starving.

Once a day this high-caste Hindoo would approach me with clasped hands, and exclaim, in Hindostanee, 'Provider of the poor, may I go and eat bread?' And then he would disappear, and for two hours was occupied cooking and eating his rice, which was a religious function altogether. When pressed with work, he would not eat at all till his labour was over.

This was a most trying event. He had been so occupied packing at Murree that he had postponed his hour of cooking till arrival at Deywal, and then the 'budmashes,' the brigands of coolies, had deserted him, and he was left all night starving among the bears and the evil spirits! This was enough to account for his misery, so I told him to go to his 'rhoti khana;' and he returned two hours after, the bright and active factotum he always was.

As the morning advanced, our baggage arrived. All the stray mules of Deywal were sent out, and in time brought in everything.

CHAPTER VIII.

CASHMERE.

CHAPTER VIII.

OUR next march was to Kohalla on the banks of the Jhellum. It is a pleasant ride down to the valley, and then through flowering shrubs and green fir-trees, and past high rocks till we arrived at the comfortable hotel, situated near the river. Across that foaming mass of troubled waters we had to pass, and then we should be in Cashmere; for the Jhellum divides the territory of the Maharajah from that of Great Britain.

There was only one way to proceed—in a flat-bottomed boat, which on inspection proved but a rickety craft. The horses and baggage crossed over in safety, and then our turn came. On entering the boat our confidence was not increased by finding a big hole in its side, which was stuffed with grass, and a large stone placed against the bundle to keep it safe !

The same performance was gone through as at Attack, on the Indus. Our boat was towed some distance up the river, and then cast off. We flew across, and made the opposite shore, some way down the stream, when, a rope being thrown, was caught by coolies, and we were hauled into smooth waters, and landed.

A fortnight after we had crossed, a brother officer, on his way to Cashmere, had passed this ferry, followed by his servants, horses, and baggage. The boat, cast off from the opposite shore, flew over the boiling, surging waters. The rope was thrown and caught by the coolies, but it was rotten, and the boat, with all its living contents, was swept away, the mad waters engulfing everything that was in this miserable old coble.

But now we are landed in the Maharajah's country. The day was far spent when we managed to start our avant guard of coolies with tents and baggage. We decided, therefore, to advance only a few miles up the mountain to a level ground, where there was water and sufficient space to pitch our tents. The ascent of Dunna is not along green sides and grassy slopes, but in the dry bed of a winter's torrent. Leaving the village where we had disembarked, the path proceeds for a short way along the level, and then straight up the stony course of the stream. My wife started on foot. With her Alpine staff in her hand, she bravely faced the hill. I rode as long as I could, but the scrambling, sliding pony was most disagreeable, so I was obliged to walk.

To describe our ascent is impossible, as no one can form an idea equal to it who has not attempted the Dunna Pass. Intensely hot in the valley, it became cooler as we scrambled and tumbled along the rocky path; and at length we arrived at the Dunna Dhuk, the only level site before reaching the top. The evening had closed in, but the moon rose clear and splendid from behind the lofty mountain up which we were toiling. The wild night-hawk's shrill note echoed through the still, dark valleys, and the light and shadow deepened as the moon rose brighter and more glorious every minute. Our tents were pitched by our active servants on a kind of terrace formed for cultivation, and our dinner was nearly cooked before we had time to look about us. Our only light was the silvery moon.

We asked for milk, and one of our Cashmerian retainers proceeded a short distance, and, facing the valley, shouted our wants in a loud and prolonged call. The answer came, weird-like, from a long way off, and, in due course, rich milk was brought to us in abundance. It was very pleasant on that cool mountain side after the heat of the plains, and we soon retired to our Swiss cottage tent to seek the repose we had honestly earned.

It was strange to awake and find ourselves encamped on the hills in Cashmere; and, when M'Kay brought us our morning cups of tea, we were ready to begin another day's march. The tents were struck and sent away, and the final orders given. My wife, as usual, faced the brae on foot, and I rode Silver Tail till I found it impossible. So I handed him over to my syce, greatly to the knowing one's internal satisfaction.

As the morning advanced, the sun's bright rays tinged with golden tints the surrounding scenery. The loving calls of the black partridges sounded sweet and home-like. The early breeze

was laden with the perfume of mountain flowers.
It was charming, but the climb was terrible. We
were glad when we reached the plateau which
overlooked Dunna, and were enabled to mount
our nags once more.

As we halted at the refuge built by the Maharajah of Cashmere, we were very thankful to take
possession of the queer habitation which he has
dedicated to the use of travellers. These refuges
are called barradurries, and have no claim to
beauty of architecture. A mud wall surrounds a
double-storied mud house. The ground floor is
uninhabitable, but a rickety stair leads to the
upper floor and into a narrow passage, on each
side of which there are empty rooms. The passage ends in a covered verandah in front of the
rooms. The doors are rough planks of deodar,
without any attempt at fastening. The window
shutters are the same, with no glass.

Many plans had to be adopted to keep the
doors and windows closed. My wife and M'Kay
made these wretched places most comfortable
with gaily-striped purdahs, and many a pleasant
hour have we passed in the numerous barradurries
scattered over the land of Cashmere. On the

right hand, as we entered the enclosure at Dunna, a tomb is erected to the memory of a young cavalry officer, who broke a blood-vessel after walking up the steep ascent by which we had come. How sad are these graves scattered over India! As the road into Cashmere no longer passes over Dunna, that memento is very lonely now. Few travellers pause to read the record of that young life's untimely end.

Very early next morning we left Dunna for Maira. The path zigzagged down through a wooded brae, and became altogether lost among huge boulders as we approached the river we had to cross. The ascent on the opposite side was steep and rugged. Clouds which had been collecting threatened a storm, and wild gusts of wind foretold rain. We got into the barradurrie, and settled ourselves comfortably. The distant thunder rolled grandly through the mountains above and around us. The elements seemed to be collecting forces for a grand attack at night, and when the darkness came the storm burst upon us, flash succeeded flash in rapid succession, and the thunder pealed forth its mighty voice; the wild wind shrieked through our mud-formed house, and drove the rain and hail into our inner-most rooms. The doors and window-shutters banged about in a mad jubilee of diabolical glee. After committing all sorts of havoc, the drunken furies flew before the gale, and the peaceful stars peeped out from the blue heavens, while the wan-ing moon shone sadly on the wearied earth. Still, in the now quiet scene, we could hear the far-off thunder echoing through the high mountains of Cashmere. These sudden storms are very grand.

The next morning broke bright and fine, and, as we rode away, the fresh perfume was sweet to us who had left the burning plains so lately. We rode through wooded, park-like scenery, aptly described by an Irish assistant-surgeon we met as 'quite like a domain.' Instead of Fenians to annoy the dwellers, there are leopards which de-stroy the poor Cashmerian wood-cutters. A day or two previous to our arrival, a shepherd had been killed. Our way led up the mountain, and then through woods; our path descended to a river which flows along the valley. High up on the hill on the opposite side was Chikar, the end of that day's march. Before crossing the river, we passed through many rice-fields, which, as they resemble wet bogs, are not pleasant places to ride in. Numerous cheerful-looking peasants were engaged planting bunches of green grass in rows in the wet and muddy ground.

After climbing the steep mountain, we arrived at Chikar, quite ready for the 'doctor,' a combination of milk, eggs, and rum beat up together, which M'Kay always had prepared for us, and which seemed to increase our enjoyment of a later breakfast.

During the day we sat out on the flat roof of the barradurrie, whence the view was magnificent. In the distance we could see a far-off snowy range, while nearer was a splendid panorama of mountains cultivated at their base, with the rocky summits lost in snow and impenetrable clouds. Every now and then a great dark shadow would skim across the mountain-side, then fade away, and the bright sun would light up the green grass on hill and dale. Faintly borne on the breeze were the voices in the valley beneath, while soaring high in the air a royal eagle would pause for a moment, then swoop away and be lost to our sight.

As we were now deserted by the moon, our early start was made in comparative darkness. When the morning broke, we overlooked the valley of Jhellum. We descended for three miles, by a winding, rocky path, to the left bank of the river, and rode along its wooded bank till we arrived at Huttie. The wonderful river's roaring voice drowns every other sound, and it insists on being listened to. On the opposite side of the Jhellum is seen the road from Abottabad.

On arrival at Huttie, we found our camp pitched near the rapid Jhellum, the ground chosen by our advance-guard being the dry bed of a mountain torrent. There was at Huttie a most wonderful Tomasha Walla, who most perseveringly insisted that we should see him cross the river, a pleasure which with equal resolution we declined; but by dint of never leaving us, whether we sat outside or inside our tents, or went for a stroll, he got his own way at last, and we reluctantly climbed a cliff to obtain a good view of our tormentor. The river at this place, pent in between high cliffs, comes tearing down in great angry waves, which seem as if no living thing could for a moment contend with them.

Standing on a rock some distance from us up the river, a black figure, with hardly anything on to speak of, and grasping in his arms a 'mussack,'* fixed our attention. As soon as he saw we were looking at him, he threw the 'mussack' into the water, and followed in a trice. It was surprising to see the ease with which he battled with the waves, turning heels over head, standing almost upright, then, mounting astride of his 'mussack,' and guiding himself to the other side of the river.

His performances seemed to give unfailing delight to the inhabitants of Huttie, who looked on as though they had not seen him go through the same feats every day of the season. Of course the Tomasha Walla's re-appearance on the scene was followed by a demand for 'backsheesh.' Have not all travellers in the East written folios on the subject of backsheesh? I must add my iota to the budget. It is the most irritating of demands. Not a man in Cashmere will ever

---

* A mussack is the entire skin of a sheep or goat. In India our bhicstics (water-carriers) bring water from the wells in no other way. Bowed down under the weight of a huge mussack full of water, a man has the appearance of carrying a living animal.

accept the payment that is offered to him, no matter that it is twice as much as the service he has done requires. He will whine and beg for more, going through a string of reasons why he should get it. At last, having either succeeded in obtaining an increase of pay, or else seeing he has no chance of prevailing, he begins a fresh clamour for backsheesh. I grieve to say that our experience of the inhabitants of Cashmere proved them to be thoroughly false, utterly ungrateful, and desperately extortionate. Honour and honesty they have none. Find them out in some lie or fraud, they grin from ear to ear, never dreaming of being ashamed of themselves.

Ground down as they are by the system of perpetual oppression, we ceased to wonder at the lowness of their morals as we saw more of the working of the rule they live under. No nation in the world is taxed as the Cashmerians are (or were, for I write of 1868). Two thirds of everything is taxed for the benefit of the Maharajah, and to see that this is duly paid a host of officials are employed, who in their turn rob the unfortunate ratepayers, till (I am within the mark) I have been assured by those who ought to know that three-fourths of every man's possessions are yearly taken from him in this grievously burdened land. It was very long before we understood the small enthusiasm shown when we congratulated the people on their smiling crops and fair prospect of a heavy harvest. What matters it to them whether the produce be good or bad?—enough will be left them for their subsistence, and more for seed for next year's sowing. But all the rest finds its way, much lightened by the hands it passes through, to the Maharajah's coffers. Our farmers at home grumble, but they live in a free country—let them be thankful.

The Cashmerian sows his land, a government official comes down on his inspection visit, and desires that each field should produce so many maunds of grain. In vain the farmer protests that his land cannot yield such a crop; he is not listened to, and woe to him if to the last seer the number of maunds be not forthcoming. He is sold out—everything he has is taken from him to pay his debt to the Maharajah.

We saw this beautiful and fatherly care of a prince for his people in full form in the Lolab

Valley. We were riding past a village along a narrow path; it was getting dusk, and we had to leave our road because four or five men who were sitting down did not get out of the way. It was an unusual rudeness. Next morning we passed the same way, and there were the men still on the ground. No wonder they had not moved, even for a sahib, for their legs were bound fast and firm in stocks, there to remain till it was the Maharajah's good pleasure to release them. All that they could call their own had been sold to pay for deficient crops, but much more was still marked against them.

' Cashmere was conquered in A.D. 1587 by Akbar's brother-in-law, the Rajah of Jeypore, when the Mahomedan king of that province was enrolled among the nobles of the court; and this lovely valley, the paradise of Asia, became the summer retreat of the emperors of Delhi.'— *History of India, by John Clark Marsham, vol. i.* ' It was conquered by Runjeet Sing in 1819.'— *Ibid. vol. iii.*

' In 1846, the Sikh army having invaded our territory, Sir Henry Harding issued a procla- mation confiscating the Cis Sutlege possessions of the Lahore crown, and he annexed the Jullunder Doab, or district lying between the Sutlege and the Beeas, to the Company's dominions, by which he obtained security for our hill stations, and a position which gave us control of the Sikh capital (Lahore). The expenses of the campaign were computed at a crore and a half of rupees—which the Lahore state was required to make good—but the profligacy of the ministers and the rapacity of the soldiers had exhausted the treasury, and, of the twelve crores Runjeet Sing left in it, there remained scarcely fifty lacs of rupees to meet the demand. Sir Henry therefore determined to take over the province of Cashmere and the highlands of Jummoo in lieu of the remaining crore. Since the death of Runjeet Sing, the powerful Raja of Jummoo, Golab Sing, had always cherished the hope of being able, by some happy turn of circumstances, to convert his principality into an independent sovereignty. During the recent contest he had played the part of an interested neutral, watching the contest, and prepared to side with the strongest. When called to assume the office of minister at Lahore, he negotiated with the Governor-General as much for his own interests as for those of the State. There could be little doubt that a clear understanding regarding the possession existed between him and the British Government; and hence it created no surprise when he stepped forward and offered to pay down the crore of rupees, on condition of being constituted the independent Raja of Cashmere and Jummoo. The sovereignty of these provinces was accordingly sold to him, but it must not be forgotten that he received only an indefeasible title to that which he actually possessed at the time. Sir Henry Hardinge by this stroke of policy obtained funds to cover the expenses of the war.'*—*History of India, vol. iii.*

* Treaty between the British Government on the one part, and Maharajah Golab Sing of Jummoo on the other, concluded on the part of the British Government by Frederick Currie, Esq., and Brevet-Major Henry Montgomery Lawrence, acting under the orders of the Right Hon. Sir Henry Hardinge, G.C.B., one of Her Britannic Majesty's Honourable Privy Council, Governor-General, appointed by the Honourable Company to direct and control all their affairs in the East Indies; and by Maharajah Golab Sing in person :—

Article 1.—The British Government transfers and makes over for ever, in independent possession, to Maharajah Golab Sing, and the heirs male of his body, all the hilly or mountainous country, with its. dependencies, situated on the eastward of the river Indus, and westward of the river Rávee, including Chumba, and excluding Lahoul, being part of the territory ceded to the British Government by the Lahore State according to the provisions of Article 4 of the Treaty of Lahore, dated 9th March, 1846.

ARTICLE 2.—The eastern boundary of the tract transferred by the foregoing article to Maharajah Golab Sing, shall be laid down by Commissioners appointed by the British Govern. ment and Maharajah Golab Sing respectively for that purpose, and shall be defined in a separate engagement after survey.

ARTICLE 3.—In consideration of the transfer made to him and his heirs by the provisions of the foregoing articles, Maharajah Golab Sing will pay to the British Government the sum of seventy-five lacs of rupees (Náruksháhee); fifty lacs on completion of this Treaty, and twenty-five lacs on or before the 1st of October of the current year, A.D. 1846.

ARTICLE 4.—The limits of the territories of Maharajah Golab Sing shall not be at any time changed without the concurrence of the British Government.

ARTICLE 5.—Maharajah Goleb Sing will refer to the arbitration of the British Government any disputes or questions that may arise between himself and the Government of Lahore or any other neighbouring state, and will abide by the decision of the British Government.

ARTICLE 6.—Maharajah Golab Sing engages for himself and his heirs to join, with the whole of his military force, the British troops when employed within the hills, or in the territorities adjoining his possessions.

ARTICLE 7.—Maharajah Golab Sing engages never to take, or retain, in his service any British subject, nor the subject of any European or American State, without the consent of the British Government.

ARTICLE 8.—Maharajah Golab Sing engages to respect, in

regard to the territory transferred to him, the provisions of Articles 5, 6, and **7** of the separate engagement between the British Government and the Lahore Durbar, dated 11th of March, 1846.

ARTICLE 9.—The British Government will give its aid to Maharajah Golab Sing in protecting his territories from external enemies.

ARTICLE 10.—Maharajah Golab Sing acknowledges the supremacy of the British Government, and will, in token of such supremacy, present annually to the British Government one horse, twelve perfect shawl-goats of approved breed (six males and six females), and three pairs of Cashmere shawls.

Then come the signatures, &c., and date, 16th of March, 1846.

CHAPTER IX.

THE VALE OF CASHMERE.

CHAPTER IX.

THE heat was very great at Huttie, for we were in a hollow, where no breeze seemed to reach us, and the mosquitoes were more annoying than usual. I do not know what we should have done in the event of illness. We had no medicine to speak of but quinine, which we found very useful, for the servants constantly had fever, and the faith they had in the mysterious white powder was implicit. Villagers and coolies used to come to us to beg for a little, and we had to harden our hearts, and give to those only who required it.

Medical science is in a very backward state in Cashmere. A surgeon we met at one of the halting-places told us that he had been entreated by the head man of the district to come and see his daughter, who was suffering from a disease of the eye. Our friend went at once to the house, and found the poor girl in a terrible state. A native practitioner had taken out her eye, and, having stuffed up the place with wool, had left Nature to complete a cure, aided by a cloud of flies. The wretched girl was suffering agonies under this treatment, the whole side of her face being a mass of inflammation. Dr. —— trusted that the measures he had taken would save her life. As it came on to rain in the night, our tents were wet in the morning, but fortunately our other set of tents had been sent on the night before. We had a long and fatiguing march up and down hill, through rice fields, and over so-called bridges. The bridges consist of two stout logs, roughly fastened together with planks, with no parapets, and with gaps of several feet between, which made the crossing of a rapid stream a service of real danger to the horses and of most questionable pleasure to pedestrians.

After a tremendous climb we came to scenery which recalled home to our memories. We were hundreds of feet above the Jhellum, whose voice sounded faint and far in the depths below us.

For some miles our road lay through park land: fine trees waved overhead, ferns nestled at their roots, and the grass glittered in the sunlight, each blade weighed down by a drop of the last night's storm. A pair of eagles were teaching their young ones to fly; higher and higher they soared in the blue sky, till our eyes ached watching them. The sun was high in the heavens when we found ourselves at the barradurrie of Chikoti.

Welcome sight! this white-washed house of rest, and still more welcome the 'doctor,' which M'Kay had ready for us. M'Kay never seemed tired. Her scons were always ready for breakfast. I do not know how we should have got on without them, for we had no bread; but as long as we had M'Kay's scons we wished for nothing else, and, as we ate them, we marvelled how she had strength to come such marches and do her work so untiringly. True she had a dandy to be swung along in, but, if her coolies were lazy, she used to lose patience, get out, and run along the steep mountain path, with the swiftness and ease a childhood spent in a Highland home had given her. Her bearers, for very shame, would trot along behind her, either grumbling at this newly-developed eccentricity in the 'belattee memsahib,' or grinning at her remarkable appearance, as she skipped along from rock to rock, a tiny mug, in which she concocted the 'doctor,' strapped on behind her waist, also any article of dress my wife would require immediately on arrival. When her pack was opened, the objects she had elected to carry were slippers, brushes, comb, and sponge-bag—all ready for her mistress.

We slept the sleep of the weary that night. Four o'clock came too soon, but we never gave ourselves any time to think of the miseries of early rising, for every mile traversed before the sun climbed the mountains and shone down on us was worth very much. There was not light to see a white horse as we came into the cold morning air ; the stars were still out, and only a faint streak in the east showed us that daylight was coming. How very enjoyable those early morning breakneck rides and walks were, the fresh, exhilarating mountain breeze giving us spirits to meet difficulties which in the plains would have seemed insurmountable, the air fragrant with the breath of roses, jessamine, and sweet brier, growing in thick and wild luxuriance.

The scenery was very grand; but this was the most fatiguing of all the marches. We scrambled, struggled, climbed to the top of a rugged, precipitous path only to descend again, and, having crossed a river, we ascended to the plateau on which the Fort of Oree is situated. Built by the Sikhs, it is now garrisoned by the troops of the Maharajah.

The barradurrie is near the fort, and is a two-storied house more than usually tenanted—by fleas. As we sat out in the verandah, we were attracted by the sound of a tom-tom, and in a short time appeared some twenty faqueers, who halted in front of where we were seated, and proceeded to bivouac. These faqueers are so-called holy men; they wear no clothes, and their long and tangled locks are covered with ashes, and their faces painted all sorts of colours. A more disgusting sight than one of these men can hardly be imagined, but a detachment, such as were now before us, had a grim kind of comicality. One of them more hideous than the others possessed a queer-looking umbrella, which he planted in the ground, and then extended himself at full length —the picture of a loathsome animal. We were glad when these dreadful creatures marched away again to the sound of their monotonous music.

There is a curious rope-bridge near Oree; two ropes parallel to each other span the deep gully formed by steep rocks on each side of the river. A chair is pulled across, in which the traveller sits and gazes beneath him at the roaring waters, prepared to engulf him if the rope were to break. Happily our way lay alongside, not across, the Jhellum.

What a lovely ride we had next morning! There were rough ups and downs at first, but then came forests of deodars, through the breaks of which the snow-covered mountains showed sharp and clear against the deep blue sky. Mighty cliffs rose sheer up to our right in some places, while the Jhellum on our left roared and thundered in its narrow passage over huge rocks with such violence that it was impossible to hear ourselves speak. My wife was riding in front, and, as she turned a corner, her horse shied to the right. A weird-looking little man, with no garments on at all, and his head anointed with cinders, was seated on the ground in a shallow cave formed by a rock, thrumming on a native banjo, with a huge cat clinging to his shoulder. He looked very uncanny, and took no notice of us, but seemed quite contented with his surroundings. We were informed that he was a very holy faqueer, who had lived there summer and winter for many years, and that every passer-by gave him something. So we added a few pice to his store.

Further on a long string of large monkeys were turning somersaults disagreeably near to the high cliff's edge; but their glee seemed unending, and they raced away above us, springing from branch to branch, and moving the forest as by a partial breeze. We came to an old ruin called Pandee Ghur, covered with ivy and buried among the dense forest.

Still further on there is a splendid ruined temple called Bhumiar, which is stated to be one of the finest specimens of a familiar kind of architecture in Cashmere. At certain times of the year numerous Hindoo pilgrims come to visit it. Perhaps the detachment of faqueers we saw at Oree may have been returning from the pilgrimage. A thunderstorm which came on hurried our proceedings, and the thunder rolled grandly as we arrived at Naoshera.

Our halting-place for the night was in the barradurrie, close to the rapid Jhellum. Here we got good-sized fish, which were caught in the most primitive manner. A crooked pin fastened to a string and baited with a mulberry, was quite enough to ensure a good plate of fish. I must not forget to mention that the mulberries were in great abundance, and, when we were in Cash-mere, formed the staple article of food for the lower classes. But the peasants are not particu-lar, and devour fruit, nowise careful whether the peaches, apples, or melons be ripe or not.

We felt rather excited as we went off to bed, for the next day would bring the fulfilment of a long looked-for event, our first sight of the Vale of Cashmere. It was grey dawn when we marched away in the morning. The Jhellum sounded louder than ever, its roar preventing any conver-sation taking place, and making it expedient for us to ride on in silence. At first we passed through rugged, narrow glens, but soon we emerged into a grassy plain surrounded by high wooded hills, and, amazing metamorphosis! the loud and angry Jhellum flowed smoothly and quietly past with not a ripple on its waters.

And now, instead of rocky paths, our road was a perfect level, part of it through rice-fields. Here we met an old friend returning to the plains, accompanied by several coolies laden with trophies of the chase, and delighted with his wanderings in the mountains of Cashmere. There is a great charm in meeting an acquaintance when far from the haunts of civilized life.

After some pleasant conversation, we bad adieu to our friend, and continued our ride towards the wooded ridge in front of us, over which lies the Barramula Pass, which is some hundred feet above the plain. This was our last scramble, and when we arrived at the summit we both exclaimed, ' The Happy Valley at last !'

The top is covered with green grass and shrubs; the view is extensive over a portion of the Vale of Cashmere. You see the Jhellum, the Walloor Lake, Sopoor, and the hills enclosing the northern side. I must own that the first glimpse is rather disappointing. Accustomed for days to the majestic mountains crowned with snow, the dark, mysterious valleys through which the river foamed and raged, the Vale of Cashmere, with its green and fertile pastures, was a sudden change. But soon our eyes became enamoured with the glowing charms of that sweet view, and were quite ready to appreciate fully all its delights.

The valley at some time must have been a vast sheet of water. The whole formation leads one to think this most probable, and the exit and drain of this vast lake must have occurred when the mass of water made itself an issue near Naoshera, and, tearing through the rocks, rushed madly on, leaving behind it the gently flowing river.

The trees in the Happy Valley are the plane, the walnut, the poplar, the mulberry, and the willow; while, higher up, the mountain sides are covered with forests of deodar and pine. Fruit is very plentiful, growing wild, and consists of mulberries, peaches, apples, pears, cherries, grapes, walnuts, and melons. Vegetables are also in great abundance. The soil is very rich, and during the summer there is no climate to be compared with that of Cashmere.

If the country were fairly governed, and the

population unoppressed by tyrannical laws and in-
justice—in short, if we had retained possession of
it when it once was ours, what a paradise it would
now be!   At present the flowers and fruit grow
wild and untended, and the poor peasants are
miserable specimens of humanity.   Many a better
class farmer has said to me, 'Would that the
English were our masters!'   When the traveller
reaches Barramula, he is in the actual Vale of
Cashmere.

'Who has not heard of the Vale of Cashmere,
  With its roses, the brightest that earth ever gave?'*

And now we were to change our mode of travelling—to have a rest from break-neck rides,
and to travel luxuriously in boats.   The horses
were to go on by easy marches to Srinagur, there
to meet us.   They had carried us well over the
hundred miles of difficult road we had come from
Murree.   The rocks they had scrambled over had
been very hard on their feet, and repeatedly they
had lost shoes; but I had come prepared for such
contingencies, each syce carrying with him four
strong leather boots, and whenever a shoe came

* 'Lalla Rookh.'

off, a boot was slipped on to save the hoof; at the halting-places a blacksmith could always be found to put a shoe on, and we had our own with us. The natives keep only one size, very small, and they have been known to give lockjaw to travellers' horses from paring away the hoof to fit them. The Jhellum at Barramula is smooth and broad.

M'Kay was much put out when she discovered there were no steamers, and puzzled the coolies by vainly trying to find out from them the wharf from which we were to embark. We had three boats, called dongahs. The one my wife and I occupied, a flat-bottomed boat, with very pointed extremities, was sixty feet long, six broad, and about two feet in depth. A wooden roof, covered with matting, extended about half its length, and other pieces of matting were fastened on to the sides of the wooden frame, which can be closed at night and raised during the day. The crew consisted of a whole family, who lived in the stern part of the boat. The oars were short, with broad, heart-shaped paddles. My wife and M'Kay made our gondola most comfortable. The sides of our cabin were festooned with red and white curtains. In the centre, hanging from the roof, were large mosquito-nets. During the day our camp beds were pushed out of the way, and a table took their place, on which were our books and writing materials. There was room also for an impromptu sofa of cloaks, pillows, &c.

M'Kay had another dongah, which she shared with our dogs, and the third one contained our servants and cuisine. Oh! the delicious sense of repose—after toiling for days among rocks and mountain paths, to feel ourselves resting in quiet and peace! It was sufficient, for a time, just to live, and lazily to look at the merry birds glancing past in the sunlight, and every now and then seeing them drop into the calm waters.

At first we had to cross a broad part of the river, and one of our crew stood in the bows, and with a pole pushed us along, while the remainder, in the stern, propelled us with the heart-shaped paddles. We soon reached the opposite bank, when most of the family jumped out on the path, and towed us by a long line, and so we glided past green pastures, in which hundreds of mares and foals were quietly grazing, past sedgy pools, where numerous herons arose

N

before us. They had no fear, these royal birds, protected by the Maharajah, as a heron's plume is a token of nobility.

> ' When day had hid his sultry flame
> Behind the palms of Baramoule,' *

we reached the town of Sopoor, which is built on both sides of the river, and joined together by a bridge resting on wooden pillars. Innumerable wild ducks skimmed past us, and the large mahseer rose to the flies which hovered over the mirror-like water during the still evening hour.

Before sunrise next day, we had left our moorings at Sopoor, and, shortly after, entered the Walloor Lake. It is the largest lake in Cashmere, and the Jhellum flows through it. The boatmen are very superstitious about crossing the lake. Offer them any amount of backsheesh, they will not attempt to enter it after the sun has set. The Walloor is often visited by storms and sudden squalls, and the flat-bottomed boats, with their heavy top-hamper, are not suitable for a gale of wind. So we entered the lake after sunrise. The mosquitoes were innumerable. I sat

* Lalla Rookh.

out on the prow of our boat to get a shot at the wild fowl, which crossed and recrossed before our gondola, and the mosquitoes covered my hands with white lumps and blood ; for they are easily killed, and are powerful blood-suckers.

The lake is choked up in many places by reeds and morass. Where the boats pass on their passage to Srinagur the whole surface of the water is covered with water-lilies. The scene was fairy-like. High towering around us were mountains tipped with snow, while green pastures encircled the lake. In the far distance, in our front, the fort of Srinagur rose proudly on the horizon, like the Acropolis of Athens, while on our left the heights above Manisbul Lake marked the entrance to that lovely spot, and in the hazy distance on our right, could just be seen the glaciers which show where Gulmurg, the 'Field of Flowers,' nestles, a green valley among the snow-clad hills. In the evening, we entered Shadipore, 'The Place of Marriage,' where the Scind river effects a junction with the Jhellum.

A Hindoo temple on a solid block of masonry is shaded by a chenár. Tradition says that this tree, which is situated in the middle of the river, never grows.   The boatmen drew up our squadron to leeward of a large barge not laden with violets, so we insisted on being taken to some other place.   We were accordingly moved to a fine open space, and moored to a post sunk deep in the mud.

My wife's favourite pug jumped out of M'Kay's boat at the first place where we halted, and now was nowhere to be seen.   A great hunt ensued, and we were beginning to despair of her recovery when the little black-faced beauty made her appearance quite unconcerned.   My wife was very fond of this troublesome pet, which had most endearing ways, but, like all her breed, was very selfish and exacting, her mistress often being compelled to sacrifice her own comfort to that of her favourite 'Polly,' a name bestowed on her in remembrance of the very kind donor, who was wife of the Commissioner of Peshawur.

One day at Peshawur, a tall, fine-looking Afghan made his appearance at our bungalow, and, having been admitted, entered the drawing-room, and saluting, produced a little black-nosed animal, which was Pug.   The armed warrior again saluted, and retired, leaving Polly distracted under a chair, attached to a long chain. She was soon coaxed from her retreat, and took at once to her new mistress, for whom she ever afterwards showed a sort of selfish affection.

The tall Afghan was a retainer of the commissioner. His gentle care of his sahib's children was very remarkable. He was often in attendance on them when they went out to ride or drive; a kindly, gentle warrior he seemed to be. But these Kybaries have strange customs, and one is the 'blood feud.' Like the Corsican vendetta, it descends from father to son. This man was one day in the city of Peshawur, where he saw a member of a family with whom he had a blood feud. Perhaps he regretted having come across his enemy, but the very honesty of the bold soldier may have made him feel bound to pursue his foe. Anyway, he followed the man, and on the road to Jumrood overtook him and slew him. Had he waited but a short time, he would have been out of British territory; but the deed had been done in our queen's dominions, where blood feuds are not recognised by the law. He was imprisoned and tried for murder, the punishment for which is death. Deep regret was felt for the faithful retainer, who, however, was not condemned to die, but to undergo imprisonment for life in the Andaman Islands. Alas! for this mountain warrior, imprisonment was far worse to him than death. Death he despised— but imprisonment! We must look at his position in his own light. We must remember that he was brought up in the faith of blood feuds. We must bring to bear all in his favour *now*, for soon we shall loathe his name. This Afghan mountaineer, this man who was the gentle attendant on children, who carried Pug so carefully into our bungalow at Peshawur, was the murderer of Lord Mayo!

In the evening it looked like rain, but we did not much mind. We settled ourselves in our tent-like cabin and laughed at the mosquitoes which howled outside our curtains, when all of a sudden everyone on board seemed demented. I jumped up and found the dress of a Highlander quite unsuited to a gale of wind. My wife also sadly deplored her scanty costume. The usually quiet going gondola was flying in a most distracted manner before the wind; our gray, red, and white curtains flew out like long, dishevelled

locks; our mosquito-nets jumped up and down
in extraordinary fits; our boatmen's family announced their numbers with great loudness, for
in the back part of our vessel the voices of male
and female old age joined in fiendish clamour
with those of youth and babyhood, and our dogs
barked incessantly ! On flew our dissipated and
ill-behaved, flat-bottomed barge, which had broken
loose from the bonds that bound it to the muddy
bank, and had started off on a lark, when the
sudden squall had rushed down from the mountains and shouted 'Come !' How we were ever
stopped, I know not; but, after half an hour of
great anxiety, the unwieldy and reckless, flat-bottomed barge was made fast to the muddy bank,
and we were left in peace to repair damages.

CHAPTER X.

THE MAHARAJAH.

CHOWNI—SRINAGUR—WOODEN BATHING-HOUSES—BABOO MOHAS CHANDER—OUR FUTURE DOMICILE—'ME COME UP'—OUR SHIKARRAH—SUM-MUD SHAH, THE SHAWL-MERCHANT—ANCIENT TEMPLES—THE MANU-FACTURE OF CASHMERE SHAWLS—DINNER WITH THE MAHARAJAH—A NAUTCH—THE MAHARAJAH'S 'HOOKEM'—LORD MAYO'S FETE AT AGRA—UNINVITED GUESTS—RISING OF THE LAKE—THE POPLAR AVENUE—THE PARIAH DOG—CAUSE OF THE FLOOD.

CHAPTER X.

WHEN morning broke we continued our voyage. As we had left the lake the day before, the river was now more narrow, and twisted and turned like a serpent in the green fields through which it made its way. And then we came to Chowni, which was intended by Golab Sing to be the dwelling-place of English visitors, but, owing to want of good drinking-water, was never used.

We breakfasted under the shade of a grove of poplars, and then, entering our gondolas again, we were towed up to Srinagur, the capital of Cashmere. As we glided along, we had to pass the old gallows on which many a mortal has suffered in days of yore; now it is seldom used, but during our visit to Cashmere a culprit was executed on it, and was left to hang there for days, filling the air with his horrid presence. But when we passed the gallows was empty, and a weird-looking old raven was perched on the cross-beam of the gibbet, croaking dismally to itself about the good times of Golab Sing, which were changed completely now. We had pictured this city to ourselves as a scene of ruined palaces, but all we saw were crazy wooden houses with pent roofs overlaid with earth and covered with grass and plants.

We passed some ancient temples, which seemed in their ruin to mark the difference between the rotten buildings of the present day and the massive architecture of a gone-by age. We glanced for a moment at splendid marble causeways, hanging over hideous wooden bathing-places, and dwellings erected on wooden piles close to gardens full of fruit and flowers. As we struggled up the stream, and with difficulty got under and past the wooden bridges which span the river, boats like our own, but not so large, shot by us. In some were reclining the English sahib, exploring. In others, larger and more crowded, were soldiers, country people, and busy-looking men. On each side of this centre thoroughfare of the town were men and boys swimming and bathing. Not a house but had a wooden bathing-place, and these were always full of splashing human beings, while crowding the banks were female figures washing clothes and children alternately. We swept past the Maharajah's palace, the golden roof of its temple being the only attraction there.

Leaving the last bridge, called Ameeri Kudal, we came to a wider part of the river, and the place where the visitors' bungalows are situated opened out. It was a pleasant sight, the calm and placid Jhellum, on the right bank of which were grand chenars—the Oriental plane—over-shadowing the curious little houses built for the accommodation of the Maharajah's British guests. As we toiled on, a swift and smart-looking gondola drew up alongside, and the Baboo welcomed us in the name of His Highness the Maharajah of Cashmere.

Baboo Mohas Chander was a courteous, smiling man. When he spoke, his white teeth sparkled in the sunlight, but, when he ceased to address us, a sudden darkness seemed to overspread his face, all because the Baboo had shut his mouth. He informed us our house was ready, and we found him always civil and attentive.

Ah, me! what a house! Our future domicile was like a square box divided in the centre, the division being the floor of the upper story. Up a rickety stair we ascended to our three rooms. The windows had no glass, but had diamond-cut shutters, the peculiarity of which was that, when tampered with, they invariably fell on the toes of the unwary. However, we were delighted with our apartments. Hearing the sound of riders passing by, we rushed to the window; the effect of which energetic movement was to make everything in the room dance, as the floor was very elastic.

As we gazed on the river so near us, and watched the gondolas skimming past, we became aware that a crowd had assembled in front of our house. 'Me papier-maché man—me show you fine things—*me come up.*' 'Me Soubona jeweller—very cheap—*me come up.*' 'Me leather man—me bring shot-bags, sandals—*me come up.*' 'Me shawl man—very fine, very cheap—*me come up,*' and so on, the 'me come ups' becoming really alarming by the constant repetition of the words. So I assumed the attitude of a popular candidate for parliamentary honours and requested them to 'retire till a future occasion,' and, finding they were losing time, they vanished.

Gradually the boats, riders, and pedestrians became fewer, night came on apace, and we were glad to say 'Good night.' Next morning we engaged a shikarrah, a miniature of the boat in which we had come up the river. It was thirty-six feet long, by three and a half wide, and one foot deep. Our shikarrah had a flush deck and awning. The crew consisted of six men, who propelled the boat with heart-shaped paddles. These craft, which are used by everyone like gondolas at Venice, seem to fly through the water. My wife and I reclined on rugs and pillows, and gave the word to proceed to Summud Shah, the great shawl-merchant. The entrance to this great man's house is by a flight of stone steps, which are washed by the river. Through a fine gateway we passed into a courtyard, and then, ascending stairs, we were ushered into the shawl-room. Summud Shah received us arrayed in an ample gown, like a night-dress. He could not speak a word of English, but by his courteous actions seemed to say : 'All I have is yours—if you pay me well.' We were handed to chairs placed on a divan, and then business began.

What a collection of magnificent shawls ! But oh, how wearisome ! Our host gave us Ladok tea, which is not unpleasant to the taste. Instead of cream, a slice of lemon floats in the cup. Summud Shah was the banker at Srinagur, and was most attentive to our wants during the whole of our stay in Cashmere. We saw two kinds of shawls. Those made by loom, and those by hand.

Some time after this visit, we were wandering through a poor part of the town, when we observed a number of men with very weak eyes. Our guide informed us that these were workers of Cashmere shawls, and that the work they were engaged in was the cause of the weakness of their eyes, and in some of total loss of sight. We visited some of their houses, and found them occupied sewing the graceful patterns on small patches of canvas. When these are completed, they are all united together, and form the beautiful shawls, some of which we had been admiring. We were also told that, when the shawls were first introduced, the inventors were in the custom of ascending the hill above the town, from which there is a fine view of the Jhellum, winding and turning in the valley beneath, and that the tortuous pattern of the Cashmere shawls is a copy of the river's windings.

I received an invitation to dine with the Maharajah. My wife was also asked to accompany the Resident's party, to see the fireworks which were to be exhibited in the evening. So far as dinner was concerned, there was amply sufficient to eat and drink, but on an occasion of that sort one goes with rather a wish to be introduced to the host. My experience of that one dinner party did not afford me an opportunity of having that desire gratified. We had been requested to come camp fashion, which means that each guest is expected to bring his own plates, knives, forks, tumblers, napkins, &c. I landed at the mean and dirty entrance to the palace, where the shouting boatmen seemed at war with each other. I clambered up the steep stairs, but there was no one to receive me, or to show me the way. I found myself at length in a large dining-hall, in which some eighty khitmegars were making as great a noise as the boatmen below, each servant endeavouring to secure the best place for his master.

After getting past this pandemonium of waiters, I was shown a door, through which I proceeded to an open terrace, where a number of chairs were placed in a semicircle, many of them already appropriated by other guests like myself—their occupants being officers on leave from British territory—so I took possession of one of them.

In the open space in front of the seats two or three nautch girls were going through that dreary and unmusical performance called a 'nautch.' In the meantime, I discovered some old friends, stranded like myself. At length, as, somehow or other, everybody intuitively knew that dinner was ready, a rush was made towards the door. Excited khitmegars seized their masters and dragged them to the place they had secured for them. I was charmed to find myself situated between a brother officer and an old friend I had not met since the Crimean days. The table was groaning with really a good dinner, for everything had been placed on it at once. The champagne was Cutler's best, and our little coterie had our dinner and jokes in a very pleasant way. We had some fun about the Maharajah's hookem (order). I wanted a glass of iced water, and I desired my servant to bring the water, and pour it into my silver mug. A great man, clad in red, came behind my chair and informed me 'that it was the Maharajah's hookem (order) that the tumblers were to be taken to the water, and not the water to the tumblers.' Verily it was a jovial party. Then the Resident rose, and proposed the health of the Maharajah. We cheered uproariously. Some one then proposed the health of the Resident, 'the representative of our beloved Queen,' we soldiers cheering loudly for our sovereign, more than for her representative. The costumes worn by His Highness's guests were peculiar; some appearing in uniform, others in evening dress, while a number wore ancient shooting-coats which bore testimony to hard work among the mountains of Cashmere.

Had the head constable of Agra been present, he would have been sorely puzzled. That functionary was on duty one evening at the Taj, when the Governor-General, Earl Mayo, gave a fête, with kind hospitality, to the residents at Agra. Several uninvited guests had tried to enter the precincts of Viceroyalty on a former occasion, and a police officer, by order of the civil authorities, determined that these intruders should not force their way again into a private party given by the Governor-General.

'How shall I know the guests of his lordship?' asked the anxious constable.

'Allow no one to enter who is not dressed in uniform or in evening costume, like Mr. T——,' replied the police officer, pointing to the officiating collector, a tall, handsome man, dressed as an English gentleman.

In the evening we were all assembled in the garden near the gate, where a sound of voices in altercation was heard at the entrance. The police officer proceeded to inquire into the disturbance, and found, to his dismay and our delight, that Mr. A——, one of the leading swells in Lord Mayo's suite, had been stopped because he had a coat differing very much from Mr. T—— ; in fact, a political costume.

The weather was so fine and warm that we decided on pitching our camp not very far from our rickety bungalow. The site where our tents were placed was on a green knoll, on whose flat surface our whole encampment found ample room. There were trees dotted all round us, and a straight path led down to the river, where we usually embarked.

For a day or two after our change of quarters the sun shone brightly, and there was a balmy breeze blowing; but it came on to rain suddenly, and never stopped doing so for thirty-six hours. Our tents were thoroughly waterproof, but to say the best of it we found our space rather confined, and the time hang somewhat heavily on our hands. My wife was sitting in the verandah of our tent, and I was not far off smoking a cigar. For some time I had observed the water round a tree gradually rising, and in a lazy kind of manner kept watching it growing deeper and deeper, and felt very pleased that we had pitched our camp on the green knoll, and not in the grass field below us. All of a sudden a native *employé* of the Maharajah came running from the landing-stage.

'To the boats, sahib—to the boats! The Maharajah has sent three—the river is rising.'

We could not understand what had happened,

but to hear was to obey, and then a wild scene of excitement ensued. Everyone began to pack up something; the servants struck the camp; M'Kay was everywhere, working hard. The only unconcerned man was an orderly sent by Baboo Mohas Chander, who was placed at our disposal when we first arrived at Srinagur. This valiant warrior divested himself of all his clothes, and, wrapping them in a bundle, squatted in a way which is possible only to natives, holding over his head an umbrella made of broad leaves. He had fixed his position at the edge of the green platform on which our tents were pitched. His apathy was very irritating to M'Kay, and she managed, when flying from one place to another, to give our sepoy a gentle push, and bundle, man, and umbrella rolled down the bank into the water.

At length everything had been transported into the dongahs, which resembled the craft in which we had travelled from Barramula, so the same arrangements held good as those which we had adopted in our former boats. Our horses had been moved at once up to high hills, and they were in safety. To our repeated question,

'What does all this mean?' the answer was astounding. The river was rising from some unknown reason, and the great danger was that
the embankment, which prevented the lake from
overflowing its boundaries, might give way, and,
if such an accident happened, the whole valley
would be inundated.

Yes, the river had already risen twenty feet,
the green bank on which our tents had been
pitched was gradually becoming covered with
water. The path along which we had hurried
was no longer visible. The flood was entering
our old, rickety bungalow, and the walls soon
collapsed like a building of cards. It was a
strange and anxious position to be placed in, for
there was nobody to tell us what to do; our real
danger was unknown. My wife and M'Kay
having made our big boat quite comfortable,
we trusted ourselves to the care of Providence,
whose good angels had watched over us in many
an equally momentous adventure.

The afternoon passed and the river was still
rising. The rain, however, ceased, and evening became night. Our boats just floated on the waters.
The moon rose in its splendour, and the still-

ness of the hour was only broken by the howling of homeless dogs, and that fearful sound—once heard, never to be forgotten—a house crumbling to the ground. Then all was quiet again, and we were left to imagine scenes of death and dismay, which in time proved to be too true.

When morning broke, the sun shone forth on a scene of desolation. 'The waters covered the earth.' There was no trace of gardens left. Many of the visitors' bungalows had subsided, and all of them had some depth of water in the lower floors. Our boatmen poled us along through places which, two days before, were dry land, and into gardens, over which a mass of water was tearing. Our crew aided their progress by holding on to cherry-trees, and freely helped themselves to the fruit, which a few hours previous they would not have reached without the aid of a ladder.

We passed through the poplar avenue, one of the walks near the city, the tall trees of which had been planted by the Sikhs many years ago. Now a torrent rushed along the favourite ride. As we glided on, we saw a poor Pariah dog seated on a door, floating anywhere, and howling piteously. My wife was most anxious to save the forlorn animal, and made the boatmen take us near to it. She spoke to it kindly, and coaxed it to be good; but when its enemy, man, came nearer and nearer, it distrusted us, and sprang from its door, and was swept away. As we looked on the vast expanse of waters our wonder was great; but how much was it increased when we both saw a rat and a serpent swimming close together, too intent on getting to dry land to take any heed of each other. As we continued on, we picked up a chicken, which was in great dismay, but soon fraternised with us, and, being named Nourmahal, became our companion for a long time after she had been saved.

It would be tedious to enumerate all our adventures. It was an experience never to be forgotten. We spent several days in our boats, but it was some time before the waters subsided, and the full extent of the damage to life and property could be ascertained. The peril most dreaded—the rising of the lake and the bursting of the water-gate—when the town of Srinagur would have been, most probably, swept away, and the whole valley destroyed, was mercifully averted.   A broad embankment is built for protection, and the water-gate is so formed that, when the lake rises, the gate closes itself; but when at its proper level the huge wooden doors open.

Our crew brought our squadron to anchor at the base of Tukht Suliman, on whose sides our horses were picketed.   We climbed to its summit to the little temple where King Solomon once sat, so says tradition.   The view of the valley is the most extensive that can be had, and from where we stood we saw the full length of the poplar avenue of magnificent trees.   There are in all one thousand seven hundred and fourteen trees, of which one thousand six hundred and ninety-nine are poplars, and fifteen chenars (so I find noted down).

The scene presented to us was most interesting.   Very many dongahs, like our own, had taken refuge here, out of which appeared mothers with children in all states of undress.   These poor ladies, like ourselves, had been obliged to embark in a hurry, and found, no doubt, that a nursery was an in-convenient obstacle to overcome.   But, like true women, they bowed to the inevitable, and made the best of everything.

We remained a few days near the friendly rocks, till the waters had subsided. During that time the great Baboo Mohas Chander had often paid us visits. He informed me that the cause of the flood was the melting of a glacier in the mountains, which had forced its way in volumes of water down to the river. I never heard this information contradicted, so I suppose it was true.

CHAPTER XI.

VALLEY OF THE SCIND.

CHAPTER XI.

THE weather had quite improved again, so we determined to proceed on our travels once more, and, having still retained our flat-bottomed gondolas, we gave orders to our new crew to take us through the drogjun, or water-gate, into the lake, whose embankments had caused so much alarm to the Maharajah and to everyone. How enchanting it all was! We had left our moorings in the afternoon, and the glow of the fading day was like a halo over mountain and woods.

Our destination was the Nishat Bagh, one of those fine old palaces built by one of the Mogul emperors. On our way through the clear water of the lake, we passed the floating gardens laden with melons. On every side were lotus-flowers and singhara plants. The lake was like a great mirror, in which the high mountains were re-produced. We landed at a flight of steps, and, mounting them, found ourselves in the terraced gardens among flowers and cherry-trees laden with fruit.

The Maharajah comes out occasionally from his gold-roofed dwelling in Srinagur, and is taken up the lake in his grand barge, landing at one or other of these summer habitations to spend the day. An order from our Resident can gener-ally secure the use of rooms in any of the palaces for officers on leave. The rooms are bare; some of them quite open to the balcony overhanging the garden. Here we established ourselves for a time.

As we were idly gazing from the verandah, an arrival attracted our notice. It was that of a native arrayed in garments of gorgeous colours; but what was most remarkable was a large em-broidery in silver on his shoulder. For some time we were greatly puzzled by this ornament; but, having got my glasses to bear on him, our delight was great to find the word 'Superfine' written on it. This conspicuous ornament was no doubt the English manufacturers' mark of the quality of the cloth in which this strange creature had clothed himself. We hailed him as 'Superfine Joe,' at which he seemed greatly pleased, as he salaamed repeatedly as he swaggered away. When night came on, our resting-place was in an alcove not far from a marble fountain situated in the centre of the fine hall. During the hours of darkness the breeze moaned sadly through this vast apartment, sounding like the sighs of those who had once lived and loved in this almost ruined palace.

When morning broke, we crossed the lake to Nishat Bagh, where we pitched our tents under the shade of some magnificent chenars planted in the time of Akbar. Before us was the calm and placid lake, the breadth of which is here some miles. Near where we landed is the Char Chenar, or Isle of Chenars, also called Rupa Lank, or Silver Island. Vigne visited this isle in 1835, and says there was a square temple upon it; but it no longer exists. He states a black marble tablet was placed there which has also disappeared. He informs us that it bore the following inscription :—

Three travellers,
Baron Carl Von Hugel from Jamu,
John Henderson from Ladâk,
Godfrey Thomas Vigne from Iskardo,
Who met in Sreennugger on November 18, 1835,
Have caused the names of those European
travellers who had previously viewed the Vale of Kashmir
to be hereunder engraved—
BERNIER, 1663,
FORSTER, 1786,
MOORCROFT, TREBECK, and GUTHRIE, 1823,
JACQUEMONT, 1831,
WOLFE, 1832.

Of these, three only lived to return to their native country.

Seated outside our tents, the whole scene was very beautiful. The lake was dotted here and there in the far distance with boats plying from one place to another. Then, rising in proud grandeur on the opposite shore, the lofty mountains towered into the clear blue sky, while at their feet nestled ancient palaces among green trees and fruitful gardens. It was a scene of peaceful quiet, which is peculiar to Cashmere, owing to the absence of all wheeled traffic. The lovely climate of this beautiful land adds enchantment to every view.

'Oh, to see it at sunset—when, warm o'er the lake,
  Its splendour at parting a summer eve throws
Like a bride, full of blushes, when lingering to take
  A last look of her mirror at night ere she goes!' *

It is no less attractive when seen by moonlight.

'Or to see it by moonlight—when mellowly shines
  The light o'er its palaces, gardens, and shrines,
  When the waterfalls gleam like a quick fall of stars,
  And the nightingale's hymn from the Isle of Chenars
  Is broken by laughs and light echoes of feet
From the cool shining walks where the young people meet.' †

As we lingered under the shade of the green-leaved trees, I endeavoured to make a sketch, and thought I had succeeded pretty well. Seeing M'Kay pass near me, I called, and asked her how she liked my drawing. As she did not answer, I said,

'You know where that is?'

Poor M'Kay was always anxious to give pleasure to anyone, so she said, in her pleasant Scotch voice,

'Oh yes, sir; that's your bungalow at Murree.'

Alas for my fine sketch of the Cashmere mountains!

Time fled very pleasantly in our gipsy en-

* 'Light of the Harem '—' Lalla Rookh '   † 'Lalla Rookh.'

campment. The scene was occasionally varied by the presence of the Maharajah as he went past in his gilded barge, followed by his courtiers in large and picturesque boats. Sometimes we paid visits to the gardens of Shalimar, and rested during the heat of the day in Nourmahal's Pavilion. This pavilion is built of marble, and the pillars which support it are of black marble. It is in the centre of a reservoir of clear water, and there are one hundred and forty-four large fountains springing from it.

> ' Th' Imperial Selim held a feast
> In his magnificent Shalimar:
> In whose saloons, when first the star
> Of evening o'er the waters trembled,
> The valley's loveliest all assembled;
> All the bright creatures that, like dreams,
> Glide through the foliage, and drink beams
> Of beauty from its fount and streams.' *

Now all is silent. The palace is forsaken, and the gardens deserted. But, happier than our old Scotland, the nightingale is heard among the trees which surround this fairy place; although, according to a Scotch assistant-surgeon,

* 'Lalla Rookh.'

there are nightingales in our Highland homes. The surgeon being asked to describe one, he gave his impression of the lovely songster in these terms :—

'It's got a heed like a caat : aboot the beegness of a pigion; and flits aboot at night; and cries, hewt! hewt!'

We could linger no longer among the fine forest of chenars near that beautiful lake, so our camp was broken up, and we reluctantly departed for the Scind Valley. We were fortunate in having the moon to light us on our way. Very beautiful was the lake enshrined among the giant hills. As we moved slowly along, a storm rushed up, sweeping the waters into real waves. The flash of the lightning was incessant, and the roar of the thunder never ceased as it rattled among the mountains. But the storm passed almost as suddenly as it had arrived.

We allowed our boatmen to take us wherever they liked best, only stipulating that we should find ourselves halted in the morning at some suitable camping-ground for breakfast.

Sunbul was the place they selected, and there we breakfasted under the shade of some wide-spreading sycamores. There was little variety in our food. We carried with us tea, and a few tins of soup, which we only used on the march. Besides these, my wife had a small store of dainties, which only saw light on special occasions. We trusted for the rest to the fowls and eggs of the country. Potatoes and bread, which were always plentiful, we had to send for to Srinagur. Milk was abundant; but beef we never saw. Bulls and cows being sacred, we might have answered, as the Irishman did, when asked to dinner by Dan O'Connell:

'Come to dinner, a quiet dinner. Ye'll get nothing but potatoes and beef.'

'Bedad,' answered Paddy, 'I'll come. It's the same dinner I have every day—*barrin' the beef.*'

After a two hours' halt, we proceeded on to Manusbul Lake, passing through a narrow canal, and under a very ancient one-arched bridge.

The canal is about a mile long, and then you emerge into the clearest water of this most picturesque lake. In the shallow parts the lotus abounds, the leaves of which are very long and of great diameter. We saw on our left an elevated table-land, at the foot of which is the village of

Manusbul. Near this hamlet are the ruins of Bádsháh Bágh, an old palace built by Jehángir for his wife, the lovely Nourmahal. On the right, a low range of hills extends from high mountains. We landed and paid a visit to the guardian of the lake, a very holy fakeer, with a gentle, good expression of face, who is spending his life digging himself a grave. When we were there, he had tunnelled out some fifty feet, and as he was then a man in the prime of life, if he is still alive, he must have burrowed a long way in. Whatever fruit happens to be in season in the valley at the time of a visitor's advent, this holy man will give it in greater perfection than it can be procured anywhere else.

The mosquitoes were very troublesome here, so we embarked again, and floated away over the clear deep water of the lake, and finally arrived at Ganderbul, where our horses awaited us. We encamped for the night in a tope of fine trees, and next morning continued our march up the Scind Valley. The river Scind was still in flood, and two bridges had been swept away, and the waters were over the lower path, so we decided to proceed to Noonur, which is only three miles from Ganderbul, and there to halt. The distance being so short, we thought it better to walk, and never did a march seem longer than this one. There was no shade, and we were on a narrow path in the midst of rice-fields. The sun beat down piteously on the marshy ground, from which exhaled a stifling air. At length we arrived at Noonur, which is a pretty, English-looking village, nestling among fruit-trees and chenars. Our four tents were pitched under the shade of one of these nobles of the forest. The horses were picketed at a little distance off, near a walnut-tree, and a tiny stream of clear and sparkling water ran past our encampment. Here we were regularly beset by 'shikarries,' the gamekeepers of the valley.

We had reached the bear country. I selected one of these men, a nice-looking fellow, who had only one 'chit,' or letter of recommendation, but that one was most satisfactory, the writer testifying to all that was said in favour of 'Jan of Kangan.' On being asked for his other 'chits,' he said they were left in his home in the mountains—'But surely,' he added, 'that was sufficient;' and so he was engaged, and we were spared the continual announcement, 'A shikarrie waits.' Our new gillie made himself useful, bringing us any amount of unripe mulberries. M'Kay also went off into the woods, and returned with basketfuls of cooking pears and apples. We remained at Noonur some days—quiet, dreamy, unremarkable days.

One morning our honest gamekeeper was brought before me like a prisoner, guarded by three other greatly roused shikarries. They salaamed most respectfully, and inquired if the sahib had engaged this man, the prisoner, as 'Jan of Kangan.' He was not the said Jan of Kangan, for Jan of Kangan was the man who now addressed 'your royal highness, the provider of the poor.' This fellow was a common coolie, who had stolen Jan's 'chit'—here were the others to prove what he had said was not true. The false Jan was speechless, and had nothing to say. He had not the ready wit of an Irish soldier-servant I once had, whom I found telling a most palpable falsehood. On being afterwards accused by me of saying what was not true, he drew himself up to military attention and said, 'Plase, sir, I lost my prisince of mind.'

The only drawback to Noonur was an excessively holy fakeer, who appeared at unexpected moments, gesticulating furiously, evidently perfectly mad. The Cashmerians looked on him with intense respect, and our servants told us that the Maharajah had begged the holy man to come and live with him, and had offered him beautiful presents, but the fakeer had refused his highness's offers, and had thrown the gifts in his face.

We had not had any rain for a week, so the Tickedar was summoned, and coolies ordered. Bitterly cold it was at half-past three in the morning, as we felt our way out of the tent ropes, and we were only too glad to walk and keep our blood circulating. When day broke, we had fairly entered the Scind Valley, in which we overtook numbers of flat-faced, Chinese-looking coolies, all laden, travelling generally in the employment of some merchant back to Ladâk.

At first the path was good, but we were soon in difficulties. The river had carried away one part of the track, and in others the water had overflowed and then receded, leaving a most slippery road. So there was nothing for it but to ride our horses into the river, the Scind, which had covered the whole of the low ground. At last we had to retrace our steps, clamber up the mountain-side, and hit off another approach to the bridge. Many misgivings assailed us when about a mile from where our guide told us was Kangan. We saw what was evidently a sahib's horse grazing, and its syce squatting on the bank opposite to us. We asked him why he was there. He did not dare to face the waters, he said, so he was waiting till the river subsided, or till his sahib returned. On we rode beside the foaming torrent to a place where it widened into three branches. The chokedar called a halt; we had arrived at the bridges. There were two very rapid rivers to cross, which we had to do by wading, and then the main body was bridged. A native went first, and, although the waters surged around him, he was able to hold his own against the tide.

So we followed on our horses. Having crossed in safety the two branches, we then came to the bridge, a pile of loose stones on either side, round which the waters madly rushed. It supported a frail ladder, turfed over in some places, the sods kept down by heavy stones that weighed the trembling structure down to the waves. However, M'Kay must have got over, for there was no trace of her, and our advance-guard of coolies and servants had also certainly managed to get across. We dismounted, and handed the nags to their respective syces. Nila climbed the pile of loose stones supporting the bridge like a cat, and fearlessly followed the syce over the troubled waters, hopping over holes in the neatest possible fashion. But Silver Tail, more impetuous, made a rush at the stone-work, to the vast alarm of his syce, who saw the near approach of a watery grave, and held on with all his might to his charger's head, shouting for assistance. But at length they both got over all safe. My wife held on to one end of a stick, while the chokedar had the other end firmly grasped in his hand. She landed all right from this swaying structure, which had no parapet, and through which the furious flood was plainly visible beneath.

In my opinion the dogs gave us most trouble in our efforts to get over this rickety structure. We were all rejoiced when we were assembled on the Kangan side of the river, and, when everything was fairly over the bridge, we continued on our way to where our tents were pitched under the shade of some walnut-trees, and where M'Kay was ready to receive us with the welcome 'doctor.'

The valley of the Scind is narrow, but the scenery is very grand and beautiful. On each side rose lofty mountains whose summits were covered with snow, and whose precipitous sides are clothed with forests of deodars. Lower down chestnut, sycamore, and walnut-trees take the place of those giant firs. Villages surrounded by cultivated land are sprinkled here and there on the banks of the river; fruit-trees afford a welcome shade, and the green carpet of grass a pleasant place on which to pitch the wanderer's camp. We enjoyed our luncheon very much, for in honour of the occasion my wife produced some of her most precious stores, and we had among other dainties a Stilton cheese and a bottle of milk punch; so we decided to devote the remainder of the day to rest and quiet enjoyment under the shade of a huge walnut-tree.

I smoked a cigar, while my wife, by the aid of my glasses, examined every nook and corner of the high mountain which towered above us. All of a sudden she exclaimed, 'I see a bear!' and there, far up on the hill-path, a bear and her cub were plainly seen. It was a pretty picture, for the mother was playing with her child, rolling it over and running away, then coming back and falling down, while the little cub jumped over her. Well, I did not go after them. Perhaps the milk punch and the cheese prevented me; anyway, I left them alone, but a brother officer, arriving soon after, encamped not far from us, and he went and shot the cub and then the mother, but nearly lost his life in doing so, for the old bear was so furious when her cub was killed that she charged my friend at a moment when his rifle was not loaded. Fortunately for him, however, another sportsman came up to the rescue, and Bruin received a bullet which finished her.

There were several bears seen during our halt at this charming camping-ground. I went out several times to shoot, but was not successful. My shikarrie generally got me out of bed about three in the morning, and we sallied forth by the light of the moon, and climbed up one of those steep mountains on which my wife had spied the mother and child. The bears came down during the night from their haunts in the mountains to feed on the ripe mulberries in the valley.

My shikarrie's plan was to take me up the mountain before dawn, and to post me behind a rock where the bears were likely to pass, as they always returned up the mountain from the valley when the day broke. I may safely say that, on these occasions, I never saw a bear. A strong smell of a menagerie was sometimes perceptible, and the broken branch of a mulberry-tree would give evidence that Bruin had been there; but I was never fortunate enough to get a shot at one. I think the fur of the American bears finer than that of the Cashmerian ones.

CHAPTER XII.

THE RESIDENT OF CASHMERE.

Q

CHAPTER XII.

WE left Mamur and encamped at Gond, intending to proceed to Sonamurg, but I did not feel at all well, so we had to give it up. The scenery had become wilder and grander at every turn round each rugged cliff, and then the mountains seemed to close entirely, so that there was apparently no possibility of getting further on, till a turn of the path led us to where the valley widened into a green enclosure. On our way we got lots of apricots, the trees being fairly weighed down with their yellow load.

Gond is a very wild place. Our tents were pitched close to a brawling stream that clamoured so loudly as it hurried past to join the Scind that we could hardly hear ourselves speak. My wife, accompanied by the dogs, proceeded alone for about five miles up the valley. She brought back a glowing account of glorious combinations of mountain, wood, and river. The intense stillness of the place imparted a feeling of solemnity to the scene. While my wife was on her way a figure appeared, at first wholly unrecognisable, face burned red, and hair a perfect thatch, dress indescribable. This was an officer of the Connaught Rangers. How amazed I was when my wife returned to our camp with this singular-looking being. He had been to Leh, and was full of stories of his adventures. He had walked thirty miles that day. As he had left his servants behind, we made an impromptu bed for him in our spare tent. He told us he had seen a state prisoner at a fort called Tillet, a man tall in height, cramped up in an iron cage where he could not sit upright. My friend measured this cruel prison, and, as far as I remember, his conclusion was that it was only four feet high, and narrow in proportion. The poor man had been immured there for years. At the time of the death of Gholab Sing (the father of the present Maharajah) the prisoner plotted to raise another branch of the family to the throne, his intention being that the prince who now reigns was to have been slain. The plot was discovered, and the unhappy author of it was condemned to a life-long incarceration in an iron cage. It is so long ago since the story was told on the valley of the Scind river by this wandering Ranger, that now my written description of the event seems quite tame; but at the time his portrait of the unfortunate wretch he had seen, and the measurement of the cage which he had marked on his stick, made us all thrill with horror, and we made a fresh inroad on the fluids in my wife's stores. I hope my friend had no difficulty in getting off his boots, as I might have chaffed him as I was once chaffed myself.

In the Crimea, during the last winter there, my old friend and comrade, Nat Steevens, and I built, with the aid of one of the Rangers, named Hopkins, a very good man, 'a moighty foin house,' consisting of two rooms, divided by a very thin partition. Nat resided in one room, while I was possessor of the other. Nat said to me one morning:

'I always can tell when you have been dining out.'

I innocently inquired, 'How ?'

'Because,' said Nat, 'I can hear you say to your servant, on your return from one of those festive parties, " *Schnopkins*, pull off my boots !"'

We had great difficulties in procuring any food, and at length I had to send in to Srinagur, to Baboo Mohas Chander, requesting him to give me a Sepoy orderly, to get us supplies. After his arrival, we did better; for we got what there was to be had—small, half-fed sheep—but we had to pay double for everything, owing to our new attendant. I do not believe the peasants gained by the change; for our 'Gascon captain,' as we named him, was a great swaggerer, and pocketed most of the money himself.

We had to cross the Scind river twice, on our return journey, to enable us to get to a better path than the one we came by, and we met with no mishaps till we reached a tributary of the river. It came brawling down from the mountains, a goodly sized stream. My wife was walking, and Silver Tail, with the side-saddle on, was being led by the syce. They came to a rickety bridge, where the impetuous pony, as usual, made a rush. The syce checked him, but down went Silver Tail into the water, and rolled twice over in the flood! The knowing rascal seemed rather to enjoy it, and swam to a shallow place, where he coolly began to drink, allowing the alarmed syce to catch him. Not a scratch was on him, nor was the little demon strained in the least. My wife's saddle was, of course, very wet, but uninjured.

We arrived early at our camping-ground at Mannur, and M'Kay started off on an expedition up a mountain at the back of our tents. It towered up many thousand feet, and from its summit a view could be obtained over the ridge on the other side of the Scind Valley, right away to Srinagur, Gulmurg, and Baramoula.

It was some hours before M'Kay rejoined us. We had seen her, through my glasses, climbing steadily on ; and, when she returned, her account of the splendour of the panorama she must have gazed on was short and pithy.

'There was nothing to be seen at the top but more mountains, and villages. As to the wonderful height, there was not a mountain of the lot to be compared in size, or anything else, with the mountains at the back of my father's house in Sutherlandshire.'

The heat in the valleys was becoming oppressive, so we determined to move up to higher ground. We turned our steps, in the first place, towards Srinagur, there to make all arrangements for a protracted expedition. Baboo Mohas Chander strongly recommended us to retain the services of the Sepoy, so the Gascon captain remained with us. We left Srinagur by boats on a lovely moonlight night, and drifted down the Jhellum with little aid from our crew. The tinkling sound of zitaras, mingled with laughing voices, came on the breeze, and added to our enjoyment as we floated along, inhaling the perfume from the flowers in the gardens on the banks of the river. The grim old temples, black with age and decay, were softened in the moonlight, and the squalid wooden houses appeared almost cheerful as seen in that sweet evening hour.

In the morning, we entered the Walloor Lake, and crossed over to our landing-place at Palhallan. The mosquitoes were more voracious than usual, and positively attacked our mosquito-nets in millions, but, baffled in their attempts to come through, they howled outside. From Palhallan we walked to Wangan, where the horses met us, they having come round by land. Our Gascon captain was in great force, and swaggered about, trying to get coolies. His moustache had an extra curl, and he proved—by his overbearing ways—a great addition to our importance, as every article of food was charged nearly double to us. Our other retainer was a chokedar, full of conceit, and what the Americans call *bounce*. When we landed at Palhallan, this man buckled on his sword, and swung my gun, in its leather-case, over his shoulder, arming himself also with a long pole, on which he fixed an old Union Jack belonging to me; and marched with pompous gravity in front of our party, greatly to our amusement, but not much to our edification.

As we passed through a village, the little naked children rushed forth clapping their hands and shouting: 'Ho! tomasha wallah. Ho!' To be taken for a party of travelling jugglers increased the delight, but not the dignity of the wanderers. Before daylight the march was begun, and when morning broke we had left the low land, and were beginning the ascent of the real mountains. A slight shower brightened everything. The note of the cuckoo, so home-like and sweet, the fir-trees refreshed by the rain, the balmy, bracing morning air, all made our hearts rejoice. We toiled up through pine forests, among which were many fine deodars blasted by lightning. We arrived in due time at Baba-murchi, where we were met by two of my brother officers, who were looking out for us, and welcomed us with the intelligence, 'We have breakfast ready for you,' a most satisfactory meeting. Need I say how we appreciated the meal provided for us by these two kind friends, one of whom now rests in his grave in India; but we were longing for news of the outside world, not having met any-one in our brief halt at Srinagur. They told us of rumours of disturbances among the hill tribes near Peshawur, always an anxious report for officers on leave, as, if anything serious breaks out, it means recall to the plains. However, the air of Cashmere makes one look on the bright side of things, and it was with wills resolved thoroughly to enjoy our holiday as long as it lasted that we got on our horses and proceeded on our way.

For two or three miles our road continued ascending through pine forests, but at length, like

> ' Lord Lovel's brier-er-r,
> It couldn't get high-er-r,'

so we began the short descent to the Vale of Gulmurg. Gulmurg means the 'meadow of flowers,' and in few places in the world except Cashmere could such a pleasant spot be found.

The long, narrow green valley, on whose sweet grass many mares and foals were grazing, is traversed by a clear stream of pure water. On each side of the valley are high broad banks, on which grow lofty deodars. On one side the bank goes up, still covered with pines, till it joins the hill behind it, and then it rises upward and upward till it reaches the line where the snow always lies. In snug nooks above the valley were to be found various tents.

Gulmurg is the most favourite resort for the less adventurous visitors to Cashmere. It was a pretty sight, for the encampments were many, and each one had some decoration, either of arbours or flags, to enliven the scene.

We had some difficulty in finding a good camping-ground, for a rather large terrace was required, not only for our own accommodation, but also for our retainers and the ponies. At last we were satisfied. For some time we had ample occupation in arranging our gipsy camp. Our tents were cosily pitched beneath some giant deodars, more than sixty feet high. It occurred to the syces, both good men, whom I had had in my service for long, that the ponies might be led down the valley to enjoy a good feed of grass. It was an unlucky thought, for no sooner did the nags find themselves in the neighbourhood of the mares than, casting decorum to the winds, they squealed, and kicked, and pranced most gallantly. The men held on to their charges as long as they could, but at last I saw the discomfited grooms prostrate on the ground, and our excited horses tearing away after the long-tailed denizens of the valley. It was next day before they were recovered. By many a bite and cut, we saw that their advances had not been too well received.

When night came, the scene was very picturesque. The large fires, always lit, near every camp reminded me of old campaigning days. We had our huge log fire, and the moon rose soft and silvery from behind the dark woods, a bright gleam occasionally piercing the gloomy darkness of the thick forest, which loomed grandly between us and the cloudless sky. It is like a dream recalling these pleasant hours, for the inevitable discomforts are all forgotten, and memory reproduces the bright side alone.

One of our favourite excursions was to the end of the valley by which we had come in, and then into the woods, along a narrow path through lordly pines, to an open vista made by the Resident. The view was very beautiful; the far-off mountains were often hid in mist, but sometimes at sundown the lofty Hurra-Mukh showed his snowy head, and the clouds faded away like a veil lifted from his god-like brow. Then the magnificent ice-clad giant, flushed in the rosy sunset glow, quickly shrouded himself again in a covering of impenetrable clouds. Beneath us was the green plain, through which the broad Jhellum shone like a band of silver, and the Walloor Lake seemed but very small indeed.

Villages were dotted here and there. In the far distance a gleam of light showed Srinagur's Fort and the golden-roofed palace glistening in the sun's departing rays.

Our constant companion was a large Thibetian dog—poor fellow, he always kept at a respectful distance, but followed us on all occasions, fascinated by our lady pack of canine charmers. He appeared to have no master, and we were told that he was the self-constituted guardian of the mares, which graze everywhere at Gulmurg, against the wild beasts that prowl down from the heights above. We liked the shaggy old dog, which never came too near; but one day we missed him, and were told that this honest old watch had been shot, so his troubles were over.

It must be difficult for the keepers to know to whom the different horses belong. Most of them are the property of the Maharajah, but some are not. I suppose they have a distinguishing mark.

The Resident of Cashmere, Colonel Cracroft, was most prince-like in his ideas of hospitality. No one could be more courteous and kindly than were both he and his wife. They endeavoured in every way to promote our amusement and good-fellowship. A hearty welcome was given to everyone who was bid to their hospitable board. Cricket was established as well as archery; polo was also greatly patronised.

Time flew gaily among the woods and flowers of Gulmurg. It was a pretty sight to see the care-takers of the innumerable mares and foals call their horses home at the fall of day by the sound of a long-prolonged cry which the guardians gave. A stampede ensued, and from hidden nooks and glens numbers of mares gallopped towards the man whose voice they knew. Some moved with a long stride, while others cantered quietly, followed by their little foals. From our green hill it was amusing to note the different manœuvres these wild horses went through. They formed up in troops, and changed front in a compact form. The place to which they had been called was not enclosed, but was at the entrance of the valley, and no straggling was allowed, owing to the dread of wild beasts. One day I saw a great number of vultures collected in the valley immediately in front of our position; with my glasses I could see that a poor little foal had died, and that its carcase was being devoured by these horrid foul scavengers of the East; but my disgust can be imagined when through the same glasses I saw Polly, the pug, enjoying herself quite as much as the gorged carrion crows. If there was not a row soon established at that de-testable feast, it was not the fault of our servants, for the Gascon captain, chokedar, and syces, led on by M'Kay, charged down among these festive guests. Polly was seized, and washed, and rubbed, and if anyone had been ill, and wanted castor oil, Polly, if she could have spoken, would have informed any inquirers where most of the bottle had gone to. Polly was a very greedy little animal. At a croquet-party given by Gene-ral Dunsford at Peshawur we were all deeply engaged showing our science at that now obsolete game, when, happening to turn round, I saw the pug on the table, surrounded by strawberries and sugar, which she did not appreciate, but up to the eyes in a large jug of cream, which had been provided by our hospitable host for his guests.

On a knoll in the valley, across the clear run-ning stream, a little church, constructed of deo-dars and green branches, had been erected. Here every Sunday a small congregation assembled, aud it was very touching to join in the service in this far-off beautiful land. The clergyman was chaplain to the 79th Highlanders, and he took great interest in his little church in the vale.

We were going one Sunday to the morning service, when we passed on the way a young horse with a broken leg, a very pitiable sight. The poor animal was trying to hobble along, its fore leg, which was broken, hanging powerless. The poor beast was evidently suffering great agony. A message was sent off at once to the native in charge at Gulmurg, but his answer was that he had received no *hookem* to destroy the horse. So Colonel Macpherson, of the Ghoorkas, took the case into his own hands, and the suffering animal was shot. The Hindoos are very careless about animal suffering though they avoid taking their lives. I have often seen at Cawnpore a worn-out camel lying all alone near the river Ganges, a small supply of food beside the forsaken beast. It is impossible to imagine a picture of desolation more complete than the dying camel alone on the river's bank.

We made many excursions from Gulmurg, once to the range of mountains one thousand feet above our valley. The path was very steep, but we were rewarded when in about two hours we arrived at Killun, another plateau above Gulmurg. But our route was higher up, and we passed banks covered with every kind of wild flowers. The breeze was cold as it came over the ice. The view of the valley and the distant Thibetian mountains was very splendid. Beneath us was green Gulmurg, with its white tents dotted here and there. Above us were glaciers and perpetual snow. In a shaded nook near the frozen stream we established our bivouac; a *pâté de foie gras*, together with some black bottles, was placed in the snow, and, in due time, we enjoyed a luncheon fit for a king. One of our party naïvely remarked that after luncheon in these high altitudes the ground seemed to rise towards him. We had no attendants with us, so we helped ourselves. Gipsy life, like campaigning, makes servants forget the required polish of every-day life.

In 1858, the Rangers marched into Lucknow. A brother-officer and myself were dining with the Commissioner, Sir R. Montgomery. My friend was seated between the hostess and another lady, and was making himself very agreeable, delighted to be in ladies' society again, after wandering about the country for months in pursuit of rebels. Dinner over, dessert was discussed, when, to my friend's dismay, his servant, who had been campaigning with his master, stole gently behind his chair, and, with great care, placed beside his plate an old black cutty pipe and a ' screw of cavendish,' wrapped up in a piece of old newspaper.

The murg of Killun is too high up to be frequented as a camping-ground ; supplies are very difficult to be got, everything having to be carried up from the bazaar which the Resident had got established for the necessaries of life at Gulmurg. Rain is more frequent there than lower down. But, all the same, it is a capital place for a picnic. We often dined with the Resident and his wife, whose camp was pitched high up on the green hill which overlooks on one side Gulmurg, and on the other the Happy Valley. Our departure after dinner on dark nights was remarkable, and like a triumphal procession. The 'Gascon captain ' and the ' Chokedar ' were both in attendance with blazing flambeaux of pine wood, which burn like lamps, owing to the liquid turpentine which they contain.   One preceded us, armed to the teeth, while the other followed, with his head all wrapped up to keep out the cold air. Occasionally a difference of opinion arose between the rival light-bearers as to the correctness of the path to pursue.   The ponies usually decided the question by taking a line of their own, and the joyful welcome of our four dogs proved that the log-fire we had been making for was the right one.   We were struck by the absence of small birds.   The woods are silent during the day, but at night large owls scream with a weird and mournful sound.

Much as we were enjoying our life at Gulmurg, we felt, if we were thoroughly to explore the Valley of Cashmere, there was no more time to linger; so reluctantly the order was given to strike tents and to move on.   We returned to Srinagur for a few days before starting again on another expedition.   Great part of our time was passed in Summad Shah's shawl-room, where we chose some beautiful shawls for friends at home and for my wife.   Nothing combines lightness with warmth so perfectly as a chuddar—there is no more comfortable dressing-gown than a choga, the ordinary dress of a better-class native. Of course, we had an immense deal of bargaining to go through, but we had a fair idea of what we ought to give both for shawls and dressing-gowns. On the true Cashmerian principle of no business transaction being possible without 'backsheesh,' the chief man of our boat's crew anxiously, and apparently as a matter of course, watched our purchases, he being entitled to a percentage on the same, and so also was my bearer. My wife, too, claimed that a something should be thrown in with the shawls, and Summad Shah presented her with a pretty silk many-coloured, hand-worked table-cover. I think all parties were satisfied.

CHAPTER XIII.

TRAVELLING IN CASHMERE.

CHAPTER XIII.

THE Khansama having announced that his part of the preparations for a fresh start were complete, after dinner on a fine summer's evening, our squadron of boats left Srinagur. We had decided on paying a visit to Islamabad. Our crew, as usual composed of a whole family, towed our big boat up the winding river. Had we gone by land with the horses, we should in an hour have done what it took us by boat much longer to accomplish, the river twists and winds in such a tortuous manner. This is the part of the Jhellum that we looked on from the heights of Tukht Suliman, and whose serpented bends gave the idea for the well-known pattern on Cashmere shawls.

At night, as usual, we halted, and in the early

morning continued our voyage, towed against the stream. We passed the day in a truly lazy manner, enjoying the balmy breeze as we glided noiselessly along, all Nature basking in soft repose. We passed green woods and rocky eminences, every now and then sighting the road. We got fresh fish from men who had merely to take the trouble of casting a net and hauling up lots of one-pounders. We came to a picturesque ruined village, all in decay, once the capital town of Cashmere, named Avantipore, after King Avante Verna. We passed under a fine old wood bridge at Bajahara, and floated past ruined mosques and gardens—for once upon a time it was a place of vast repute.

On the second day, in the afternoon, we arrived at Kunbul. There was more than usual fuss at that landing-place, for a great English lord was about to embark for Srinagur, and all honour was to be shown to him, by order of the Maharajah. Owing to this redoubtable party, we had some difficulty in getting coolies, and the 'Gascon captain' had to twirl his moustaches and look very fierce before we could get our proper number. My wife and I walked on in the cool evening hour. Our road was along the banks of a stream hid by flowering shrubs and long grass. The fields looked well cultivated and green.

It was a pleasant walk, and we soon arrived at an orchard of fruit-trees, underneath the shade of which our camp was to be pitched. A venerable old fellow, the head man of the village, came up to us, and with profound salaams conducted us to our ground. In the twinkling of an eye the place was swept clean, and then began the clatter of tent-pegs being knocked into the ground. The servants placed every table and box in exactly the same corners of the tents as they had occupied when our camp was pitched at Gulmurg. No life can be more comfortable when travelling than camp-fashion, make as long or as short a day's journey as you like. You sleep on your bed in your own room, and are waited on by your own servants. Now, however luxurious and well appointed an hotel may be, you have not your own odds and ends round you; the waiters do not know your ways, and the pillows are sometimes distracting.

We passed several pleasant days at Islamabad, making excursions in the neighbourhood, and visiting the various objects of interest in the town. There is a palace here, called Sirkari-Bagh, in which the Màharajah and his ladies repose, on their way to Srinagur from Jumrood. It is not a very interesting building, but there is a nice fruit garden, surrounded by a high wall.

The Barradurrie of the town is close to the Anut Nag, and is encircled by a high wall, which encloses a vast space about sixty or seventy yards square. The sacred spring, Anut Nag, issues at the foot of a hill which overlooks the town, and is received into a tank, from whence it flows through a canal into a lower tank. It then continues its course by another canal to the outside of the high wall, where it rushes forth in a fine cascade about seven or eight feet high. The tanks and canals are full of tame fish, which are regularly fed by the faqueers, and are considered very sacred. The Sonur Pookur is a stone tank, not very far from Anut Nag, and the stream which flows to it has its source in the hill overlooking Islamabad. There are two other streams, one of which is sulphurous. The medicinal properties of this mineral water are peculiar in their effects.

The Barradurrie is a picturesque, though not over clean-looking wooden edifice, round the entrance of which numerous curious faqueers establish their bivouac. We preferred our camping-ground, and remained there.

Whilst here, we visited a shawl manufactory, the entrance to which was situated in an unwholesome quarter of the town. The perfume was not that of roses, and the workers were miserable-looking objects, with sore eyes. It was curious to see these squalid creatures employed at that intricate work, which in time produces shawls of great value. The small squares shown to us were of most beautiful fabric, and no doubt the weak eyes which gazed on us got the lacklustre look from hard work at the looms. The rugs and carpets made at Islamabad are much cheaper than those sold by the merchants at Srinagur, though in reality most of them are made here. We bought several handsome hearth-rugs, besides a long, warm blanket, called 'loué,' peculiar to Cashmere.

The old tickedar was very civil, and brought us to his house, where his wife and daughters came and gazed with smiling faces at my wife.

After a great deal of good-will dumb-show, which reminded me of the 'Bono Johnny' of old Crimean days, we left the delighted family open-mouthed with admiration.

The environs of Islamabad are very pretty. There are pleasant rides through gardens near the river, and a long avenue of poplar-trees extends for more than a mile through green pastures.

Next day we determined to visit Atchibul, where there is a beautiful pleasure-garden, laid out by the Emperor Shah-Jehan, and we were told there was a summer-house in the centre of the grounds, where we could rest. The charm of our gipsy life was that we were enabled to start whenever we pleased. My wife and M'Kay made all arrangements for a picnic, and the amiable tickedar provided coolies on the shortest notice to carry our food. As our expedition was only to last one day, the tents were not struck. When M'Kay brought the tea at an early hour, we anxiously asked how the weather was looking, and felt proportionably delighted when we were informed that it was very fine. Clouds had been gathering the day before, and rain appeared imminent. We mounted our horses, and sallied forth. M'Kay accompanied us on foot, all our dogs, plus two puppies, came also. Our way lay through the rather dirty town, and we were very pleased when we emerged from narrow lanes to green orchards in the open country.

After crossing the river, we followed the right bank along which the road continued. Then our path lay through rice-fields, very treacherous to ride over. Our horses constantly sank in the boggy ground. In front of us were mountains, whose summits were covered with dark clouds when we started, but, as the day went on, rain and fleecy mist succeeded the lowering curtain, and, as if by magic, the mists faded away, and left the clear outline of the green hills painted on the autumn sky. As we advanced on Atchibul, a hill clothed with young deodars rose grandly before us, and, as we approached the gate of the gardens, we passed under magnificent chenars. The entrance is rather formal, but the Pavilion, situated in the centre of a tank of clear water, is very charming.

A civil old fellow bade us welcome in the name

of the Maharajah, and, after bringing us some fine peaches, left us to ourselves. In a short time the *jets d'eau* which surrounded us began to play, and continued doing so all the time we were there. The day was warm, as the sun had conquered the clouds, and the splashing music of the waters was soothing and thoroughly Eastern. The old gardener brought us grapes, peaches, and plums, so we passed a few hours very happily, having brought a supply of books. The fruit which is to be got in India is not equal to what we have cultivated at home in hot-houses. There are, of course, certain fruits peculiar to the country, such as mangoes, bananas, and oranges, which we cannot surpass, but as a cart-horse may be a very fine animal, yet in refinement cannot be compared with a thorough-bred, neither can the natural produce of the soil be compared with the highly-cultivated results of skill. In Cashmere there is an abundance of the fruits of the earth when they are in season. No high walls and locked doors are required to keep out thieves, or to prevent visitors from wandering about among the extensive garden-paths.

But at home it is different. A friend of mine

in the south of Ireland was taking some ladies to
see his very fine hot-houses. When they reached
the garden, the door was found to be locked, and
the key was there, but in the inside. Great perplexity was felt on the part of the Irish host how
to get in. He shouted to the gardener, and a
voice answered, but not much to the purpose.
There was much excitement and confabulation as
to how the party outside the walls was to be admitted. Finally a happy thought struck the
master. 'Whisper, Pat!' he shouted, 'throw
the key over the wall, and we shall let ourselves
in.' So, with many a 'Stand clear—are ye ready?'
whiz the key came over the wall, and, with considerable triumph, our friend said, 'Now we'll get
in!' It had never occurred to any of them that
the easiest way would have been to unlock the
door on the inside.

Several notabilities of Islamabad came to pay
their salaams, among them a Sikh officer from
Peshawur, who went into ecstasies about the
place, and concluded by saying, 'Oh, if the
English were possessors of this land, what a
paradise it would be!' The hill which rises in
the background is covered with young deodars,

which the Maharajah preserves most strictly, and which add very much to the quiet beauty of the scene. In the time of the Emperor Shah-Jehan, when this pleasure-garden was trimly kept, when the cascades were full of water, and everything was cared for, this place must have been unsurpassed in loveliness. The spring of water in this rare old garden is considered the finest in Cashmere, and the water sparkles in its clear purity when poured into a glass.

Atchibul only requires careful looking after, for the ground is fertile ; peaches, quince, plums, and grapes grow in abundance in its orchards. The day was far spent as we rode away, and as we passed through the curious gate which divides Shah-Jehan's garden from the outward world we both exclaimed, 'How often shall we look back with pleasure on our day at Atchibul!' Our path homewards was the same by which we came in the morning. The shades of night had closed round us before we reached the camp.

Our next picnic was to the wonderful ruins of Martund. M'Kay was left in charge of the camp, and we started in the morning towards the village of Bowun, which is about six miles from our ground, on the northern side of what is called in Cashmere a kuraywah, or table-land. These kuraywahs vary in height from three to four hundred feet, and in length from one to five miles. They are divided from each other by wide ravines, through which flow mountain streams. The upper part, which is generally bare and flat, is composed of very rich soil. The scenery is not very grand, and the path skirts along the foot of the kuraywah, on which the temple of Martund is built.

In due time we arrived at the sacred spring of Bowun, whose holy waters are received in a large tank full of tame fish. On the one side of this tank is a temple, from which emerged a very holy man, in search of backsheesh. We did not respond to his appeals, but a stout khansama belonging to an English family in Cashmere, seemed a great find; for he had to pay for every-thing. First he was mulcted of his coin to pro-vide food for the fish, then he had to pay before he was allowed to kneel down to try to embrace a fish, which, as he was stout and rather old, I need not say he did not succeed in doing. I then saw him paying for admittance into the temple, to be blessed by the holy man. The last I saw of him was when he was surrounded by little boys shouting for backsheesh. The limp state of his money-bag, however, showed that he had no more to give.

Yet why should we laugh at this poor Hindoo. It was faith that carried him on, faith as powerful as that which inspires the pilgrims of Russia to leave their homes, and crowd the Church of the Sepulchre at Jerusalem, and the same faith as that which caused the martyrs of old to smile as the fire was lit to consume their bodies. Magnificent old chenars are near the sacred spring.

There were so many faqueers here that we determined not to halt, as these gentlemen are not particular about wearing any clothes, and despise soap and water. We declined all offers of a guide, for our ancient tickedar had provided us with a coolie who knew the road. So we turned our backs on Bowun, fully convinced that Nature was most bountiful to this beautiful land, but that man ruined it by extortion and folly.

We proceeded by a very steep path to the top of the kuraywah, on which are the ruins of

Martund. The view was fine. Iu the far distance we saw the woods of Atchibul on one side,
aud in front the green entrance to Kunbul.
Martund is a wonderful place. Vigne says in
his 'Travels in Cashmere,' 'As an isolated ruin,
this deserves, on account of its solitary and.
massive grandeur, to be ranked, not only as the
first ruin of the kind in Cashmere, but as one
of the noblest among the architectural relics of
antiquity that are to be seen in any country.'
And what did we see? We went out on a calm
summer evening on a rocky coast, where Nature
had cast about in endless confusion great rocks
of ponderous size; that is what we seemed to
see, but these massive blocks of stone and
masonry, tumbled about in magnificent disorder,
once on a time formed walls surrounding the
temple. The temple still stands, in spite of the
loss of its surroundings, which have succumbed
to the gales and storms of ages. It rears its
noble front in proud grandeur and disdain of
overwhelming and destructive time. We entered
this ancient edifice through a gateway. It seemed
to us to be built on a cruciform plan. The aisle
was there, and, towards the east, the altar recess,

while at each corner the cross was completed by projecting spaces like chapels. On the walls of stone were strange figures cut, but the roof in most parts had failed, and the blue sky formed the canopy overhead.

There was something pathetic in finding ourselves alone in this monument of bygone days. Those who once worshipped in this very grand building must have been some of the great ones of the world, and now their very existence is unknown. The knowledge of who they were is but dimly seen through the ages of the past. Were it not for these grand mementoes which outlived the memory of those who worshipped in them, who now would think of them?

We prepared to pass the hot hours of the day in this sacred retreat, delighted to be left alone to our thoughts, which must, under the circumstances, be somewhat solemn. Our hopes of solitude were doomed to disappointment, for, entering the portals of the temple, a salaaming figure advanced, and, having arrived at a respectful distance, squatted down on the ground before us. He was a young, well-dressed Pundit, and, as we were actually reposing in a Hindoo temple, we received him courteously, though, like many callers, his absence would have been preferable to his presence. He observed that the ruins were very large, to which undoubted fact we, of course, agreed. He produced a long roll of parchment signed by many names, and pointed with pride to the signature of Vigne. This roll had belonged to his father. He then brought out several 'chits' or characters, and requested me to give him one. Being rather puzzled what to write, I looked over the numerous sheets of note-paper, one of which particularly attracted my attention. 'This is to certify that Pundit—is the greatest bore and nuisance I ever met. Signed ——.' They were all to the same effect. Having never met this worthy man before in my life, and being most anxious to get rid of him, I wrote, 'This to certify that Pundit—is the son of his own father,' and signed it. He received this certificate with great pleasure ; but, as he did not understand a word of English, I cannot make out what good he could possibly derive from it. I bowed him out, as is the custom in the East, and sincerely hoped we had seen the last of him.

We passed a very quiet day, and when the

sun began to sink to rest we prepared to leave this grand old monument of ancient Cashmere. We sallied forth from the venerable ruin, and who should be there but the Pundit? He said a good deal, but all I could make out was back-sheesh. So we gave him a small silver coin, and he asked for more, 'as his day was spoilt.' The quiet and the calm of the time-worn temple was forgotten, and with wrath we turned away from this extortionate beggar, and, with ruffled tempers, began our return march to Islamabad. Instead of retracing our steps to Bowun, we continued along the kuraywah on which Martund is built. After riding for two or three miles, we descended a steep path and entered again the road on which we had been in the morning.

As the evening was very close, we dismounted, and, seating ourselves under the shade of a wide-spreading tree, we made our syces take the horses to a clear, running stream close to our resting-place, and our thirsty nags enjoyed a cool drink. As there was no water to be had at the temple, a coolie carried a serai of drinking water for us. But the shades of night warned us to loiter no longer, so we remounted, and soon found ourselves once more in our pleasant camping-ground.

Our time in Cashmere was drawing very near to its end. We began to count the days of our holiday. One more expedition we resolved to make, to the Lolab, said to be a beautiful and fertile valley, situated on the north-western side of Cashmere. As the way to it was partly on our return journey, we sent off our horses to meet us at Sopoor. Our return to Srinagur was un-eventful. We floated down the stream from Kunbul, where we embarked. There seemed to be a calm everywhere, and, as we stole past gardens, the perfume of flowers came to us on the breeze, and the sound of children's voices was toned down to music by distance. We remained a day or two at Srinagur, during which time a grand parade of the Maharajah's troops took place, and his army nearly came to grief, for somehow or other the ammunition in one of the men's pouches took fire, and a most extraordin-ary scene ensued, as the fire went down the whole of one of the ranks, and some men were badly wounded. I daresay the men would do well enough if called on to fight, but their ideas of discipline are different from ours.

It came on to rain one day, and a sentry posted near where we were taking shelter coolly took off all his clothes and waited till the storm was over till he dressed again! Baboo Mohas Chander came to see us, and looked quite sorrowful at our departure; but he showed his white teeth with delight when we expressed our hopes of returning some day to Cashmere. He gave us some skinny fowls and a tray of sweetmeats, and then vanished from our sight. In all probability I shall never see the Baboo again, and can say with truth that he always was most courteous to us and attentive to our wants. But oh, how we loathed the skinny fowls! The very sight of chicken was enough to make us shudder. Now in England a chicken is a delicacy—not so, however, in Ireland.

Many years ago, the dépôt of the Rangers marched all through Ireland, and we never could get anything to eat at the inns on which we were billeted but cock and bacon. At length we really had cock and bacon on the brain. It was always our question, on arriving at the inn, when the waiter appeared, 'Pat, what can we have for dinner?' and the invariable answer was, 'Anything yer honour chooses to order.' 'Well, then, we'll have a roast leg of mutton.' 'Faith, sorr, there's not a sheep been killed for the last month or two.' 'Oh, then,' we frantically exclaimed, 'roast beef.' 'Sorra a bit of beef at all, at all.' 'What *can* we have?' we all shouted in despair. 'Cock and bacon, sorr,' triumphantly roared our present tormentor.

Fish at Srinagur was very difficult to be procured. The large mahseer are coarse food, and no fish were allowed to be caught between the two bridges on that part of the river on which the palace is situated, as the soul of the Maharajah's father now dwells in a fish. The Maharajah, who is very attentive to his religious duties according to his light, visited the faqueer's temple every day.

CHAPTER XIV.

FAREWELL TO CASHMERE.

CHAPTER XIV.

AND now the time was come to bid adieu to Srinagur. In the cool evening hour we floated away, under the bridges and past the old temples, till we came to Sopoor, where we found our horses, and our tents pitched. Next day commenced our last wandering in Cashmere. It was a fine bracing morning when we rode away to Arwun, where some iron-works have been established. We went through green fields and orchards and vineyards; a cool breeze tempered the heat of the sun. But a thunderstorm came on, with a gale of wind, which lasted but a short time, leaving us, however, rather dishevelled. Our path next day still continued through fields and orchards, and then we climbed a steep hill, at the other side of which was a good road, which brought us to Kundee, amid scenery that recalled the Alps.

Next day we continued our journey to Lalpari, where we found a house, in which we took possession of some empty rooms, and established ourselves for a few days. The weather was very good all the time we lingered here, and the walks under the shade of the fruit-trees in the cool and invigorating air was a strengthening tonic before beginning again the busy scenes of military life in the plains.

During one of our rides, we came on the camp of Colonel Bright of the 19th Regiment, who, with his wife, was enjoying a *dolce far niente* existence in the green valley before returning to work once more. The regiment to which the colonel belonged had been associated with the Rangers in many a quarter at home and abroad. Officers and men of both corps were sworn friends, and during the Crimean campaign the 19th, 77th, and 88th formed the left brigade of the light division, and were like one regiment.

It was a pleasant feature among the old battalions of the *ancien régime* the friendship which existed between them, and which feeling had descended for years like an article of faith. On the other hand, animosity, that sometimes existed between two regiments, was also an hereditary feeling. There is one corps now, under some new name in Her Majesty's army, which never meets with the 88th without a serious row among the men from a feeling of hostility which began in the Peninsular war.

We made the most of our days in the Lolab, for we well knew that it was the last scene in our Cashmerian experiences, and most thoroughly we enjoyed our remaining hours in that peaceful, beautiful valley. At last the time came for us to start on our return journey. We met with no special adventures on our way, and after ten days' march we found ourselves again cordially welcomed at Colonel Brown's house at Murree.

The cart to take us down the hill to Rawul Pindee had been secured weeks before our arrival; for at the close of the leave season there is always a great rush for conveyances. A Murree cart is a very low, strong-built dog-cart, with canvas roof, most suitable for bad roads. They are usually well horsed with a pair of strong ponies, which travel at full speed, and accomplish the distance down in four hours.

At Rawul Pindee we chartered a dawk-gharry, and after the inevitable difficulties occasioned by unbroken horses refusing to start, we arrived at Nowshera, where we once more began the busy life of soldiers in the plains during the cold weather. It was the middle of October, and the weather was very pleasant. The thermometer in the verandah at 4 p.m. stood at 78°, in the drawing-room 66°. But during that season there was an immense deal of fever in the Peshawur valley, two-thirds of the regiment suffering from it. It was just the ordinary prostrating Indian fever, not by any means of a deadly nature. The men went to hospital for a few days, and came out well, though weak.

When M'Kay announced one evening that she had got 'the fever,' we thought nothing of it; she was so strong and sturdy. It was only the doctor's imperative orders that made her remain in bed; she was so unwilling to leave her work undone. But instead of shaking off the fever as others did, and getting up at the end of a few days, she sank, and, before we quite realised the calamity that was threatening us, she was gone. Her death was a real grief to us; she had so thoroughly identified her interests with ours that we felt we had lost a friend. The sergeants of the 88th volunteered to carry her to her last resting-place in her grave at Nowshera, far from the home in the Highlands of Scotland she was so fond of.

We had only a year to remain in India before our turn for home service came round, and one day the order was received that the 88th Regiment, Connaught Rangers, was to hold itself in readiness to proceed to Kurrachee. The years we had spent in India had been passed in the north-west provinces and the Punjaub, and we all regretted that our last year of Indian service was to be in the Bombay Presidency, as it entailed the necessity of parting with our carriages, furniture, &c., before we set out on our long journey. However, we had no choice, and Indian fashion-lists were made out of all our possessions and sent to the regiment that was to succeed us at Nowshera. Carriages and horses were advertised in the papers, and it was with the barest necessaries of life, minus even our fine tents, as I had accepted a good offer for them, and had borrowed two from the commissariat for our march to Loodiana, that we rode away before the regiment to our first camping-ground at Akhara. I there received a telegram from head-quarters changing our destination from Kurrachee to Agra—a most welcome order, had it come a little sooner, as the sale of our possessions would not have taken place, and present loss and future expense would have been saved to every one of us; for carriages, horses, and furniture were all required at Agra. However, as it was, we were glad to hear we were to have another year in the north-west provinces, and in such a good quarter as Agra.

In former marches, during the Mutiny time, a number of elephants were attached to our battalion, but now we only had camels. The former were very amusing to watch; their ways are so peculiar. When I went to visit them on the line of march when halted, the mahout in charge would shout out to them 'salaam!' and then all their trunks would go up in the air. These great animals were each fastened by a thin chain bound round the hind fetlock, and attached to a tent-peg, driven into the ground. I have been often amused to see how much they disliked flies or mosquitoes. When troubled by these tormentors, they would take up a lot of dust in their trunks, and throw it on their backs, and give a gentle little squeal, which, coming from such a huge frame, was intensely comical. I have seen a mahout fearlessly leave his baby in charge of an elephant. Sweeping a space clear within reach of the animal's trunk, and placing the black child before him, he departed with the warning, 'kubbardar' (take care), which the huge creature, perfectly understanding, anxiously watched if the baby tried to crawl beyond the assigned limit, and gently swept it back with his trunk, if it did.

It was very amusing, when out riding, to meet an elephant. My horse had not the least fear of them, but some nags grow quite wild at their approach. So elephants have been taught to scuttle away on the approach of equestrians, and hide themselves. I have often seen a monster rushing behind a wall, and stand there, with its eyes just over the fence, looking as wise as possible, and full of mischievous fun. We had a goodly number of animals belonging to ourselves: horses, dogs, goats, and poultry. The goats are a necessary of life; for their milk is the only kind procured in most places in India. Their feeding is a simple business. A man goes out with a large flock of them in the early morning, and, after they have picked up a subsistence in the open country, they are returned to their various bungalows before milking time in the evening. I had, one time, a very curious goat—poor Nan—who was killed by a jackal. In the hot weather at Cawnpore, when the evening came, and all the doors and windows were opened that the weary inhabitant of the bungalow might emerge, half dead, to breathe the outer air, and to recline for a short time in one of those long easy-chairs made of cane, my goat would be sure to make her appearance at my elbow, and whisper a gentle, subdued 'ma—a!' I knew perfectly what she wanted: a good-sized tumbler of brandy and water; after drinking every drop of which, her spirits became very lively, and she danced about on her hind-legs, and really was a drunken old goat.

These were the days of hunting rebels. The

Rangers formed part of a column under command of Colonel G. V. Maxwell. The camel-corps, under Colonel Ross, Rifle Brigade, was attached to the column. We were ordered to a place called Ackberpore, there to await orders. Sir Hugh Rose was triumphantly marching through India, and then was approaching Calpee, a stronghold of the rebels not far from where we were then encamped. With our column was a civilian magistrate, who had all power to punish ill-doers in the most summary way. Ross's camel-corps was ordered away on what was called a 'dour,' or expedition in search of rebels. He marched early in the morning.

I was in my tent that same day, when some of the men of the 88th came up, leading my goat Nan, and marching prisoner a native. They stated that the man had been trying to get Nan to go with him, and that she had resented this very much, which attracted their notice, and then they recognized the colonel's goat, so they seized the robber, and brought him prisoner. Not one of us understood a word the man said, so I desired the soldiers to take the native and hand him over to the magistrate sahib. When they arrived at the civilian's tent, the magistrate was just mounting his horse to proceed on some duty, so the order was given to have the thief placed in some safe place till the official's return. I thought no more of the affair, as it was out of my hands, and old Nan was reposing close to my tent. Next morning, I received an indignant note from Ross, informing me that when the camel-corps was marching off in the morning, he had seen my goat straying away, and that he had desired one of his coolies to take it to the 88th camp and give it to the colonel sahib. The native, as I have described, had been taken prisoner, but the very sad part of the story has to come. The magistrate had not believed the coolie's story, and had ordered him to be flogged and turned out of camp. Naturally, Colonel Ross was much displeased, and I was equally distressed, but I explained matters, and sent the poor man a good present of rupees, and I received a letter saying that the coolie was quite pleased, and would willingly be flogged every day for the same amount.

The common crow or jackdaw of India is a most sapient bird. I have often watched them holding counsel together, apparently hatching plots, and the conclusion of their consultation always seemed to end in a shout of raven delight. My wife and I were sitting outside our bungalow one evening, and my old dog Nelly had either stolen or been presented with a mutton bone, which she was enjoying. Two jackdaws appeared on the scene, and hopped about in front of Nelly, evidently with a view to getting her bone; but she made sudden rushes at them, and away they flew, laughing. After a bit one of the rascally birds advanced very near, so near that Nelly thought she could catch him, and made a rush, at the same time leaving her bone, when down came the other bird to seize the prey; but Nelly was too quick for them, and got back to her prize. A fresh noisy conference then ensued between the two villainous conspirators, which chattered and laughed, and again flew away. Next time they renewed the attack, one of them danced before Nelly, while the other hopped up in the rear, and actually took hold of the old dog's tail. This was too great an insult. Nelly flew round indignantly, and pursued the insulting miscreant, when in a trice the other crow popped in and flew away with the mutton bone, old Nelly returning quite abashed, and evidently not appreciating our laughter at all.

The march down country was conducted in the same way as it had been four years ago, when we came up from north-west provinces; the heavy baggage, married people, and impedimenta going on the day before. As I have already said, we had got rid of everything we could before leaving the Punjaub. So it was with deep dismay I received the tidings that greeted us when we rode into camp at Hattee, two marches from Nowshera, that robbers from the hill tribes had come down during the night and emptied several of my boxes, carrying off my best uniform and almost all my valuables. It was inconceivable how the robbery could have been effected, as my bearer lay between the boxes that were broken into. Of his honesty I never had a suspicion. There is always, however, a silver lining to every dark cloud, and ours in this case was, that it would have been a much heavier loss if my wife's boxes had been carried off, containing, as they did, diamonds and other jewels. I may here mention that some months after the robbery I got back my blue patrol jacket, which had been found by the police in a suspected house in Peshawur; but nothing else was ever recovered, and for the rest of the march, so far as I was concerned, it did not take many carts to carry my baggage. During all the remainder of my stay in India, I was haunted with this robbery, for it seemed to me that I never asked for anything, but I was told it had been carried off by the hill tribes.

The day before we marched into Rawul Pindee we were halted at Janee-ke-Sung, near Brigadier Nicholson's monument. The brigadier was a *preux chevalier sans peur*. I have often read the inscription on his tomb at Delhi, where he fell at the siege in 1857; but he lived long enough to know that the enemy had been beaten and their stronghold taken. He was only thirty-five years old when he fell, but he had obtained a most wonderful influence among the natives of the north, by whom he was both feared and loved. There is a sect in existence called after his name, who worship his memory.

Our next halt was at Rawul Pindee, and at the wonderful *store* that provided all sorts and kinds of 'English goods,' from candlesticks to flannel shirts, I was able to replenish my exhausted wardrobe. These 'English stores' are one of the great features of Indian life. I daresay now, with a railway up to Peshawur, home goods are cheaper, but in the days of which I write everything of English manufacture was enormously dear, and there was apt to be a tarnished, spotted appearance in the goods that made their acquisition a doubtful pleasure. The merchants conducted business in a very superior manner. To appear behind their own counter was a thing unheard of. In short, ready money in those days was not the way of the country. Even the collections at church were made with slips of paper and a pencil, the money being called for next day.

I have an amusing letter in my collection from one of the store-keepers in the Punjaub. An officer in the Rifle Brigade, having ordered a forage-cap, addressed the letter to Mr. ———, shopkeeper, &c., from whom he received the following reply :—

'SIR,—I will do our best in having a forage-cap made up for you as kindly desired. I would, however, remark that we prefer not being addressed as " shopkeepers," as we have no claim to such.'

From Rawul Pindee we tramped on past various camping-grounds to Goojerat, where we spent many rupees on presents for home friends. Goojerat is celebrated for its inlaid gold on iron-work. I got a very handsome brace of pistols and various knick-knacks done in the same style. Near our camping-ground was the scene of the great battle of that name. Of course the cultivation of the fields has altered the appearance of the surrounding country. Our march along the high-road was varied by crossing the rivers of the Punjaub, which at this season had dwindled into small, deep, rapid streams, traversed by bridges of boats. But it was heavy work for men and animals getting over the wide reach of deep sand that we met with on each side of the streams. It was as much as could be accomplished in one day.

Six days after crossing the Chenab, we arrived at Shadera, and encamped near Jehangir's tomb. Runjeet Sing took away all the marble of the tomb to make the gardens of Shalimar. It is about two miles from Lahore, the capital of the

Punjaub, which stands on the opposite bank of the Ravi, and, like most Indian towns of any pretensions, looks more imposing in the distance than it does when you explore it. But Lahore is very majestic. It is eight miles in circuit, and is surrounded by a high wall flanked by bastions and by a broad moat. There are some very fine mosques here, notably the mosque of Padshah, with its lofty minarets and cupolas, and of Vizier Khan, covered with painted and lacquered tiles. The bazaars were good, and some of the work of Lahore, such as the lacquered work and the gorgeous shawls sewn with gold and silver threads, are well worth buying.

I met with a sad misfortune while halted at Shadera. We were exploring the lovely gardens round Jehangir's tomb, in which everything was in a state of wildest luxuriance. A protruding thorn branch fastened itself in my one red tunic, and inflicted injuries too deep for the most skilful tailor to be able to make a neat mend. More sorely than ever did I feel the evil wrought me by those thievish hill-tribes. Though it was only the end of February, it was getting very hot in tents, and the sun was already high before the morning marches were accomplished. The dusty encampment at Meau Meer was very disagreeable, not a green leaf or a tree near us; we had to stop here to change our carts; our last important halt before completing our march.

My wife and I let the regiment get a day ahead of us when we reached Ferozepore, as we stayed with an old friend who welcomed us most warmly. It is a pretty green station, once the British boundary. We saw here the most wonderful flight of locusts pass over the place. The whole air was darkened with them. I can only compare the effect to that of a blinding snow-storm; but the colour was grey instead of white. All the populace turned out with tin pots, kettles, drums, and tom-toms to prevent the enemy settling, and the main body passed the station in about an hour, but thousands of stragglers kept flying after them all the afternoon, and many thousands more dropped exhausted. The natives collect the fallen, and make curries of them, which is not at all a bad dish; but woe to the green fields if they be allowed to alight on them—not a blade of grass or green leaf escapes these fearful marauders.

The next flight of winged things we saw was a flock of wild geese, so numerous that the whole goose tribe seemed to be emigrating to more temperate zones.

CHAPTER XV.

THE HIMALAYAS.

U

CHAPTER XV.

IT was the 9th of March when we reached Loodiana, having left Nowshera the last day of January, and here we were at what was then the terminus of the Indian railway. We got down to Agra in a couple of days, breaking the journey at Meerut to let the men have their rations cooked, and on the 13th of March we arrived at Agra, well pleased to have reached our final destination.

The general at Agra, having been sent home on sick leave, I got command of the brigade, which I retained till the 88th left the station on their way to England. Agra is a very pleasant quarter, and although the heat was great, yet we managed to keep our houses cooler than at Rawul Pindee during the hot weather. India is so well known now that I shall not minutely describe the early morning ride to welcome the only cool breeze in the twenty-four hours, which is wafted like flowers strewn in the path of the conqueror, the sun. Nor shall I dwell on the dark rooms and the kuss-kuss tatties fixed into the window-frames, and always kept wet by coolies dashing water on them. The sweet fresh perfume these scented grass shutters gave forth was quite delightful. The day passed quickly enough, and then, when the sun sank in the evening hour, the doors and windows were all opened, and we sallied forth, pale and exhausted, for a drive, to 'eat the air' on the Mall. The water-carts had laid the dust and created a fictitious coolness. Energetic young officers cantered past on their ponies to the tennis-court. The crows sat on the branches with their beaks wide open, and the green paroquets chattered merrily and flew past like a flash of light. On certain evenings the residents at the station met each other at the band stand, and listened to the regimental bands discoursing very good music. It was wonderful, however, how everyone plucked up as the evening went on.

We were very fortunate in our domestics, many of whom had been with me all the years I was in India. I never engaged any servant who could speak English, as those who can do so are generally the worst of their class. Our communication was necessarily limited, as I never mastered more of the Hindostanee language than was sufficient to give orders. One day I found on my dressing-table the following letter, evidently written by one of the men in the bazaar who made letter-writing a profession, and who no doubt had charged my house-bearer for the same:

' HONOURED SIR,—I humbly beg to inform your honour that my mother is so apprehened in a hard illness that she cannot sit and get, and my wife will bring forth after some days. Wherefore I most humbly beg to inform your honour that, if you kindly and graciously bestow upon me the favour of leaving, I shall ever pray for your long life and prosperity.—I am, sir, &c., &c., THAKUR, bearer.'

Taking into consideration the lamentable state of his family, I bestowed the favour, and never saw Thakur again.

This letter reminds me of what took place at

Cawnpore some years before. The young Rajah
of Ulwar (since dead) arrived at Cawnpore with
a large camp. The officers of the 88th wished to
be civil to this young native prince, so a card was
dispatched, worded in the usual form: 'Lieutenant-Colonel Maxwell and officers 88th (Connaught Rangers) request the honour of his highness the Rajah of Ulwar's company to dinner,'
&c., &c., &c. My feelings may be imagined when
I received the following reply: 'Moha, Rajah of
Ulwar, and his company give thanks to you, and
excepted the dinner this evening, but requests to
distribute the rations to all men from the bazaar
as Hindoo regulation, also we are meet with you
this evening at seven o'clock, March 19th, 1864.'

The Rajah's company consisted of several hundred followers, for whom I was expected to distribute rations in the bazaar! I forget how we
got out of the dilemma, but we certainly did not
provide food for the followers. The young noble
came in a magnificent dress, covered with jewels,
accompanied by about twenty of the most fierce-
looking attendants, also arrayed in grand suits.
His highness would eat nothing, but seemed to
appreciate cherry brandy, and caused me some

anxiety, as he insisted on drinking it out of a large claret-glass.

There are many interesting relics of by-gone grandeur in and near Agra. Everyone has heard of the Taj-Mahal, but no one who has not seen it can imagine the perfect beauty of this tomb. Built as it is of white marble, in a climate which does not tarnish the purity of the stone, it rises gracefully in clear lines from its surroundings of green trees against the blue sky. But night is the time to see it, and we were especially favoured when Lord Mayo paid his visit to Agra, and gave a garden-party among the flowers and fruit-trees of this most romantic spot. The guests were received in front of a temple in the gardens, from which there is a fine view of the tomb. Suddenly a flood of brightness came from blue lights lit upon the height in the background, and the Taj stood out clear and distinct in startling beauty. Every pinnacle and cornice of the exquisite marble of that most dream-like monument of love was seen for a moment, and, as the light faded away, the tomb glided back into a sepulchral gloom.

Near Agra there is a deserted city of palaces, called Futtehpore Sekri. We drove there one evening, when the moon shone clear and bright, and the air was cool and balmy. In five hours we reached the gates of this ancient place. There was no one to receive us, for there are no inhabitants. We took possession of Miriam's palace, so stately, yet quite deserted. The moon shone on white marble walls, and the noise our servants made getting things ready for us re-echoed through the vast and empty corridors. During the night the sound of jackals' hideous laughter was strange and uncanny, and the scream of some wild bird startled the listener; no one but visitors like ourselves had rested there for several hundred years, Futtehpore Sekri having been abandoned for that period.

When the morning broke, we wandered about among massive ruins, and everything looked different in the glowing sunshine; but still no living being was to be seen, we were the sole inhabitants of the palaces. I cannot attempt to give more than an idea of the forsaken city.

Ackbar was the founder of Futtehpore Sekri, and he built it with the full intention of making it the seat of government. His hall of judgment is a curious erection, consisting of a single apartment, with a massive pillar in its centre. He was throned on the summit, and on four cross beams branching out from the centre were seated his four principal ministers to administer laws to the world. There is the hide-and-seek palace, full of tortuous passages, where the ladies of the court amused themselves. In a court near this palace is Ackbar's chess-board. The pavement is laid in squares of marble, and tradition says that the knights, bishops, and pawns were his queens. His durgah, or holy palace, is a magnificent structure, with its splendid mosque on one side, and on the other an enormous gate. In the durgah is the exquisite marble shrine of a holy man. The elephant gate, guarded by two monster elephants with intertwined trunks, has an uncommon effect. Beyond it is a tower, bristling with very good stone imitations of elephants' tusks. From this tower Ackbar used to review his troops. We had our friend, the Assistant-Commissioner at Agra, with us, and he most kindly acted as cicerone, and told us what we were looking at. In all my wanderings I never saw anything more entrancing than this deserted city. The dry climate has not touched the red sandstone of which the palaces are built, and we could imagine its streets swarming with busy life, its edifices filled with the splendour of Ackbar's magnificence. But the dream faded away, and left the reality of utter desolation.

Tradition says that Ackbar deserted his capital to satisfy the caprice of a very holy faqueer who had been in possession before Ackbar made his appearance. Certain it is that, as suddenly as they had come, kings, queens, courtiers, nobles, followers, and men of lesser degree, vanished away, taking up their quarters twenty-two miles off on the banks of the sacred Jumna, and called the place Agra.

The general commanding, having been summoned away for some reason, I got command of the division, and it became my duty—a very pleasant one—to proceed to Mussoorie and Landour, to inspect the dépôt at the latter-named station. It was no new ground to me, for I had paid a visit to Mussoorie during the hot weather of several years, and I was well acquainted with its many beauties. I was also glad to take a farewell glance at old remembered haunts. My wife accompanied me. We travelled by train as far as Seharanpore. In spite of all that has been done to make railway travelling luxurious in the hot weather, it is a terrible ordeal. The dust sifts through the closed, jalousied windows in clouds, and, swiftly as we may fly through the air, it is the atmosphere of a furnace that we breathe. Cases of heat apoplexy were so common that at all the principal stations shells were ready for the bodies of those who had succumbed, and at each stoppage a scrutiny was made of every carriage to see who required assistance. We had a huge block of ice with us to cool the atmosphere, so we arrived in safety at the end of the railway part of our journey. A dāk-gharry was waiting for us, and we rattled along the dusty high-road, past miles and miles of ripe corn-fields.

In the distance, through the haze of heat, we saw the well-remembered giant mountains of the Himalayas. Before reaching them an advance low ridge of hills, known as the Sewallic range, has to be crossed. It is a wild, jungly country. Tigers and huge snakes have their haunts in the fastnesses of the Terai. At the Mohun Pass we changed from gharry to doolies, and were borne at a steady trot by four bearers up and down, the way abounding in huge boulders and rocks. They keep up a monotonous chant as they move along, the words often applying to the burden. I was not a light weight; and ' Oh, the elephant! oh, the elephant!' was the refrain of their song, which changed occasionally to ' Oh, the great man, the great prince! Backsheesh from the great king.'

Dawn was breaking as we emerged from the pass, and apparently immediately before us, though really fourteen miles distant, towered the mighty Himalayas. A rest for a bath and breakfast at the delightful, cool, and clean hotel at the foot of the mountains, prepared us thoroughly to enjoy our steep climb up to Mussoorie. As we rose higher and higher, we got, as it were, into the very heart of the hills, and to us, direct from the breathless plains, the air seemed strangely rarefied, and gave one a sensation of deafness, which passed away after a short time. We were pleasantly lodged at a private hotel not far from the club.

After the duty was performed which had brought me away from the heat to the delightful temperature of the hills, we wandered about among many well-remembered places, not forgetting Landour, where we had passed some months a year or two before this visit. Mussoorie is the fashionable part of this hill station, but is not to be compared with Landour in purity of air and grandeur of scenery. In the early morning there is nothing to equal the view. When the sun has just risen above the mountains, and the soft breeze fans you gently, the distant sounds are heard like far-off music, and it is difficult to realize—looking down on the plains, which extend in the boundless horizon like a glistening sea—that the thermometer, which marks 70° in this mountain retreat, is registering well over 100° in the beautiful country on which you are now gazing. Then on the other side of the heights, far off in the heavens, tower the snowy range. In the world, there can be nothing more superb than the view of the snowy range as it bursts suddenly into sight, peak upon peak glittering bright and cold under the cloudless sky. There is a hitherto unknown, intense feeling of solemn awe as one gazes on the still grandeur of perpetual snow. Nearer and nearer come mountains and valleys. Down hundreds of feet below appears a silver line, so far off that it requires glasses to discover the washer-men beating the clothes with fearful energy in the stream. The mountain on whose spur Landour's many cottages are gathered, is two thousand feet higher than the one on which Mussoorie is built, and the air is so exhilarating that one feels inclined to shout out for joy. I was grieved to say farewell to this favoured spot, and often, when a cold east wind is blowing, the remembrance of Landour and its soft, sweet breeze comes back to my memory like a dream.

As we prepared to descend the mountain to Rajpore and Dehra, we had to pass the club, where we saw the well-dressed young officers lounging forth, on their way to the Mall, where all Mussoorie assembled to talk sense or nonsense, as suited the occasion. Some delicate ladies and children were in jampans, while others rode or walked.

At Dehra we got into our dāk carriage, and proceeded on our journey to Agra. Dehra is a green and wooded station, with bungalows, most of which have gardens round them; and, although sometimes fever and cholera visited the place, it was not generally unhealthy. The great attraction to many was that Dehra was the Newmarket of the north-west provinces. The stables were filled during the hot weather with horses in training for the first meeting of the season, which generally took place in October. I had a stable in charge of Henry Hackney, whose knowledge and care, added to his great honesty, made me fully appreciate his value. My stable consisted of thirteen horses, and, as the leave season began in April, I used to proceed to Dehra as early in that month as I could get away. What a pleasant time it was! Up every morning at sunrise, a light-hearted lot of fellows would meet in the stand on the race-course, and there criticise the different horses as they took their long slow gallops. When these performances were over, coffee would be discussed, and then, before the sun had dried the dew on the grass, the various members of that little coterie would disperse to their several stables to see the horses rubbed down, and to get the opinion of the different trainers. Some would then mount their hacks and gallop off up the mountain to the Mussoorie

Club, in time to eat the good breakfast which early rising and exercise entitled them to enjoy. I always liked the training season better than the race week, for the watchful interest was over when that week came round, although it was very satisfactory to win the rupees, which helped to pay the expenses of the stable.

For days before the races took place, Dehra assumed a very gay appearance. Tents were pitched everywhere, and the whole station was excited and merry; and, when the first day came, four-in-hands, dog-carts, carriages, and pedestrians assembled on the course. A week after the races were over, Dehra looked deserted, for not only had all the tents disappeared, but the leave season was past, and the Mussoorie Club empty.

The natives in India do not flock to a race-course the way our country-people do, nor do they take such interest in the sport as Irishmen did. When I was quartered at Boyle, a sporting squire had a horse called Harry Lorrequer, which was entered for a steeple-chase to be run near our barracks. A young, fresh-looking Englishman had just joined our dépôt as ensign, and the owner of Harry Lorrequer, having seen him ride, liked his seat, and fancied the way he managed his horse, so he asked the new-comer to ride for him. The young officer did not know what he was undertaking when he agreed to pilot the nag in the Boyle Steeple-chase. The day was fine, and a great crowd of countrymen, staunch supporters of the owner of Harry Lorrequer, were assembled near the temporary stand. They were all armed with shilelaghs, and were very vehement in their declarations 'that niver another horse would win' but their one. The start took place amid shouts of defiance, 'the boys' ran like madmen over the course, but Harry had it all his own way, and won in a canter. 'The boys' were frantic with delight; they crowded round the winner, seized hold of the young Englishman, roaring and cheering as if they were going to murder him, carried him on their shoulders everywhere, and at length allowed the exhausted youth to escape.

Some days after, I was driving my young friend in my dog-cart, and happened to stop at an inn on the road, when a quiet, mild-looking Paddy touched his hat and said,

'More power to ye, captin, ye rode fine the other day, yer honour.'

'Oh, you were at the Boyle Steeple-chase,' was the reply.

'Is it me, sorr?—sure I was one of the boys that carried ye round the coorse,' said the countryman, cocking his hat, and looking surprised at not being recognised.

'If I had lost the race, what would you have done?' was the question then put by my friend.

'Bedad, captin, I don't know,' replied the man, scratching his head; 'but any way the other horse would never have been let to win. Yer honour was quite safe to do it.'

My young friend's face was a picture worth seeing.

Dehra, with all its pleasant memories, has some sad ones too. That fearful scourge, cholera, lurks among green trees and dense vegetation, and suddenly declares its dreaded presence. One autumn the station was more than usually filled by owners of horses who had many stables. The hotel was very comfortable, as Mr. Williams did all he could to make the time pass pleasantly by attention to the cuisine and the arrangement of his hotel. It consisted of two bungalows and extensive stabling. My stables had thirteen loose boxes, and the whole of the first floor in one of the bungalows was my dwelling-place. Captain Dowdeswell, 7th Dragoon Guards, had a stable and lived in the other bungalow in the compound. One morning I went as usual to the stand on the race-course, and found those already assembled there in great wonderment at the severe pace. Dowdeswell was taking one of his horses round the course. As he passed the stand, I shouted to him that the coffee was ready; but he only waved his hand, and then we saw him soon after get on his pony and canter home. As usual, we dispersed, and I well remember going to Dowdeswell's bungalow in great spirits, for my horses had done their gallops very well, and Hackney was confident of success. The room opened on a verandah on the ground-floor, and I called out Dowdeswell's name, and, receiving no answer, went in, and was greatly distressed to find that he was very ill.

As the doctor lived at some distance, I ordered my trap, and went off to find Dr. Allan of the Ghoorkas, a most able man; but, although I went to different places, I failed to meet him, so I left messages asking him to come quickly to the hotel. I returned, only to be summoned to Dowdeswell's room; but he was dead. In less than four hours that dreadful disease had carried him off. These sudden shocks amid a gay and thoughtless party are very startling. The day before he was as well as any of us assembled there. The next morning we saw him take his last ride, and the following day he was in his grave!

It is surprising how time slips away in the quiet, drowsy atmosphere of an Indian hot weather. The punkah waves to and fro for ever; the coolie who pulls it sits outside in the verandah like a black machine wound up. Meals must be eaten, but it is difficult to know what to order; when the meat that comes in the early morning is unfit to be used in the evening, we fall back a good deal on fowls, curry, quails fattened by ourselves, and tinned provisions. What would the lady of a house in India do without tinned provisions? The salmon which looks so well at her 'burra khana' has journeyed from afar in hermetically sealed boxes; in some ladies' opinion,

those who have never left the shores of Hindostan, the use of these sealed dainties is quite
general in the highest society at home.

'So you dined with the Queen?' said one of
these untravelled ladies to some general officer
lately returned from Britain. 'I suppose that at
Her Majesty's table there was nothing but tinned
provisions.'

It is some years since the charming lady I
allude to made this remark. The constant communication between England and India must
have enlightened even those who have never left
the country. In the hot weather Sundays mark
that the weeks are passing; there is little else
to do so. Divine service was at six in the evening, and the pale congregation gathered under
punkahs to follow the clergyman, who, under his
special punkah, read the service and preached a
sermon. How very much hotter he must have
been than we, who were melting, I can answer
for, as I frequently officiated as clergyman in
various quarters of India, owing to the absence,
from sickness or other cause, of the padré sahib.

I remember on one occasion the clerk whispering that there were banns of marriage to be pro-

claimed, and he only handed me the names of the pair. I utterly forgot the words of the form to do this, and could not find the place in the prayer-book; then, with startling distinctness, the old Scotch formula came to my mind, which I had often heard in the days of my boyhood: 'There is a purpose of marriage between So-and-so, of this parish, &c.,' announcing the same, to the considerable entertainment of some of my hearers. Occasionally, when the heat seemed to have reached its highest pitch, the bearer would appear, and ask leave to roll up the outside verandah chicks, as a storm was coming. The air felt thick and heavy, and the breathless stillness was overpowering. In a moment all was changed, and a raging tempest was upon us. A dust-storm is a terrible sight—the whole atmosphere a red mass, a whirlwind of dust, and all as dark as night around. I have stood at the window looking out into the darkness, and felt that there was some one beside me, without being able to distinguish who it was. Then the rain came down in torrents—we sallied forth always with an expectation of finding it cooler, but the sensation is that of a hot vapour bath.

CHAPTER XVI.

OUR FINAL JOURNEY.

CHAPTER XVI.

ON the 6th of November, 1870, the head-quarters of the Connaught Rangers left Agra by train for Bombay. It was our last journey in India. I had passed many pleasant years in the country, and I had received great kindness from friends, many of whom I most probably would never see again. Indian hospitality has not been over-rated. I have been told that now-a-days there are so many railways that hotels take the place of dāk bungalows; but in my time it was different, and at the various halting-places the burra-sahib of the place generally came himself to welcome any wanderer to his own house, and to show him all the attention he possibly could think of. When I look back at the days passed in Hindostan, the names of Lind, the Commissioner, and Judge Spankie, of the High Court, stand out among a crowd of others, and re-call to my memory very happy days. So it was with mingled feelings that I bid adieu to the burning plains.

At Allahabad I had to part with my bearer. I am certain it was with mutual regret we went our different ways. I see now his erect figure marching away out of the railway-station, laden, as usual, with his beloved copper cooking-pots. He was a Hindoo, but more attentive to his devotions than many an enlightened Christian. An honest, good man like him, although a heathen, must surely have his reward. We were five nights in the train before we reached Deollalee, from whence the final departure for home is made. The train pulled up during the heat of the day, and was put into a siding, while the men got their meals cooked.

Our first halt was at Allahabad. We spent the day with my friend, Judge Spankie. Our last experience of Indian hospitality was in the house of a friend whose unvarying kindness I shall never forget. Some of the places we stopped at were merely railway-sidings ; tents were standing for the accommodation of the regiments. Our cook, who travelled down country with us, always managed to give us a tolerable dinner, making up a little mud fireplace beside the train, and, as a matter of course, going through all the ordinary dishes.

Jubbulpore is a large station, and there we got into the hotel, which was very full. A large party, newly arrived from home, were going up country, among them half a dozen pretty, fresh, English girls. When we were quartered at a certain station in India, there was only one ' spin ' in the place, and she, poor thing, received such overwhelming attention that quite inadvertently she was engaged to two men at the same time. Deollalee, where our last few days in India were spent, was an immense erection of wooden barracks and huts. Regiments newly arrived from home were halted here, as well as those about to leave the country, and the respective arrangements were made between the various departments of the in-coming and out-going corps. The servants who had accompanied us down country now left us, taking service with the new-comers.

On the evening of the 16th of November, we got into the train for our final journey. It was daylight when we descended the Ghauts, a most wonderful piece of engineering. The railway goes down a sheer fall of nineteen hundred feet, in a succession of zig-zags. Our train was a long one. The carriage we were in was at the end, and, in looking out of the window, the engine, with its following, seemed another train on quite a different line far below us.

It was the afternoon when we reached Bombay. It has left no very distinct impression on my mind, as we proceeded direct from the station to the tug, which took us off to the huge *Jumna*, that was lying waiting for us. We were fortunate in every respect in our voyage in her. The weather was perfect, and Captain Richards, the captain of *H.M.S. Jumna*, was unvaryingly kind and courteous. On the 17th of November, the shores of India faded away, never to be looked on by me again. The splendid ship we were in, with its luxurious comforts, was a contrast to the vessel in which I had come out to India thirteen years before.

Now, on our return home, we were embarked

in a magnificent troopship. I think there were seventeen hundred souls on board, but everything was in such beautiful order that there was no confusion. My regiment got on capitally, and Captain Richards reported very favourably of the men's conduct when in his ship.

1870—71 was the last season that regiments were conveyed across the isthmus from Suez to Alexandria by train. We left the *Jumna* with much regret. The train was drawn up almost immediately alongside. We started in the evening from Suez, and arrived at Alexandria about seven o'clock next morning—one man short. He got out in the desert to get a drink—as we heard long afterwards—and the train went on without him, in consequence of which he lost his home passage, as well as his train. On arrival at Alexandria, we embarked at once on a tug, and proceeded on board the *Crocodile*. One of the many children that were accompanying their parents home distinguished himself on the short trajet from the wharf to the troopship by carefully untying the fastenings of a cage-door, and letting loose a very valuable minar, which the unconscious owner had brought at great trouble to himself from the far north of India. I do not think he ever knew how his bird escaped. Minars speak most perfectly, much more distinctly and with a better imitation of the human voice than a parrot.

It is very annoying losing a pet, especially when the conviction must be that it will inevitably come to grief. I recall a curious case of the sort which happened in Scotland at my old home. My sister-in-law had a parrot, which had been the object of her care for many years. In fine summer weather, when the windows were open, it flew out, and enjoyed itself very much among the trees in front of the house, and, when called, returned to its cage. One day a sudden gale of wind came on, and the poor bird was carried away before it. A great search was made; but it never came back. My sister read in the county paper an advertisement, couched in the following term: 'Found, a parrot. Anyone having lost the same, apply to,' &c., &c. In hopes that this referred to her lost favourite, she wrote a full description of Lorry, and anxiously waited for the reply. Her disappointment was great when she received the following answer to her application : ' Milady, i am sorry to say that it was a *farot*' (ferret), ' and not a *parot*, that was found.'

The *Crocodile* was a fac-simile of the *Jumna*, with the exception of not being painted white. In the Mediterranean, we were caught in a gale, and found that the *Crocodile* was not distinguished without cause for her powers of rolling. The storm delayed us three days, as we could make no headway against the wind. It was the last rough weather we encountered, but as we neared our own latitudes the cold became intense. Nothing could have looked much more miserable than we poor denizens of a warm climate did that 21st of December, as, with eager eyes and longing expectation, we crowded the sides, and looked at the goal of our hopes for long years— home! Take the Solent on a fine, bright, sunny day in summer, with yachts and pleasure-boats glancing over the surface of the rippling water, and you will say it is a fair sight to see, but what we looked on now was a grey and leaden sky, the whole country under snow, and an occasional flake in the air, proving there was a good deal more to fall. Slowly we came into our berth alongside the quay, and it did seem a realization of our long dreams when friends and relations flocked over the gangway, and warmly welcomed us back to the old country.

The next day we disembarked. The snow that had been threatening was now falling, and it was freezing very hard. One mouth previous the sun was shining and the thermometer marked 86°. The men of the 88th, with their white-covered helmets on their heads, had, like all of us, red noses and yellow faces. We thought it was positively cruel to bring us suddenly from intense heat to bitter cold, but, in spite of shudders and chattering teeth, we all felt an exhilarating glow on that 22nd of December, 1870, when we disembarked during an eclipse of the sun and in a blinding snowstorm. The 88th regiment proceeded to Fort Grange, and that night thirty men were taken into hospital with bronchitis. The regiment did not remain very long quartered in the forts, but were moved over to Portsmouth, where it occupied the Cambridge Barracks.

What a changed place is Portsmouth now that the old walls have been removed! It has assumed a gay and youthful look. Midshipman Easy would not recognise it, and the old tars of former days would feel quite adrift. The last ten years have greatly improved its outward appearance. It was always a favourite quarter, being so near the Isle of Wight, and the young officers of the different regiments stationed in Portsmouth and the neighbourhood kept the ' tambourin a-roulin,' as no doubt they do still.

There was a good anecdote told about the subaltern of the main guard at Portsmouth during the time that a noble lord was commanding the district. A ball was to take place at the Southsea Rooms, and, as ill-luck would have it, the hero of my story was in orders for guard the very day of the ball, and could get no one to exchange duties with him. Despair filled his mind, for *she* was to be there, and he was engaged to her for several dances. Cupid, they say, laughs at locksmiths, so, I presume, goes into fits when a subaltern's guard is mentioned as an excuse for being a recreant knight. So our hero decided he would, like Cinderella, go to the ball for only a certain time. As the other officers were in uniform, his costume was not remarkable, but he kept his eyes on the general, and once, when whispering soft words into his fair one's ears, he saw his lordship give a start as he looked towards him, and felt sure he saw his lips form themselves into the appearance of a strong expletive.

In a short time the general called his aide-de-camp, and our young warrior looked out for squalls. He followed his lordship to the door, saw him get into his carriage, and heard him give the order, 'To the main guard!' Away flew the fiery steeds. On arrival of the general, 'Guard turn out!' was shouted. Everything was correct. The officer was at his post, and reported 'all correct.' This ought to have been sufficient for the visiting officer, and satisfied him that he had made a mistake, but, if all stories be true, the then commander-in-chief at Portsmouth never made a mistake, *in his own opinion.* He called the young officer to him, and asked him, 'Did I not see you, a few moments ago, in the Southsea ball-room?' And the only reply he got was, 'How could that be, sir, as I am now here in command of my guard?'

So the older wise one departed, and the younger retired to his guard-room to smoke and dream. But the affair was not over. Next morning the

A.D.C. arrived at our subaltern quarters, requesting his attendance at Lord ——'s house, and our
friend went at once. The general, I have always
been told, was very kind-hearted. He received
the young officer most courteously, and then
said,

'Mr. ——, the guard you were on is a thing of
the past. We meet now as friends. I want to
know how the mischief you ever managed to get
to your guard, for I am positive I saw you in the
ball-room.'

On receiving the reply: 'Behind your lordship's
carriage !' it may be imagined how the general
laughed, and, no doubt, was of opinion that the
young officer had shown a great deal of clever-
ness in getting out of what might have been a
serious scrape.

This escapade recalls to my memory a story I
heard given by a most amusing *raconteur* in Scotland. The colonel of a regiment quartered in
Edinburgh Castle had been much annoyed at the
number of men who not only were brought up
to the orderly-room for drunkenness, but also for
absence without leave, so he was determined to

make an example of some one on the first opportunity.   One morning the regiment was on
parade, and a private soldier appeared with his
coat all muddy and his cap in a battered condition, quite sober, but evidently having been
engaged in a row, and 'absent all night.'   Here
was a 'horrid example.'   So the colonel ordered
a corporal's guard to make the man a prisoner,
and, forming the regiment in line, he marched
the culprit in front, so that every soldier might
see him.   On arriving at the left flank of the
line the prisoner saluted, and said, 'Thank you,
colonel; it is one of the finest regiments I ever
saw. You may dismiss them,' which rather altered
the colonel's intentions with regard to this 'horrid
example!'

I would like to command a regiment formed of
officers like the Portsmouth subaltern and men
like the Edinburgh private, although neither of
them, I daresay, knew anything about Spenser's
'Faerie Queen,' a knowledge of which is required at
examinations for commissions in the army of the
present day.

But I must finish now.   At Portsmouth I said

farewell to my dear old home in which I had passed all the years of my soldiering life, and now again I say God speed to you, old 88th ; luckier than most time-honoured corps, you are Connaught Rangers still, but full of bygone memories are the numbers 88, the sound of which has echoed in peace and war, at home and abroad.

THE END.

LONDON: PRINTED BY DUNCAN MACDONALD, BLENHEIM HOUSE.

MESSRS. HURST & BLACKETT'S

LIST OF NEW WORKS.

LONDON:

13, GREAT MARLBOROUGH STREET, W.

MESSRS. HURST AND BLACKETT'S
LIST OF NEW WORKS.

THE FRIENDSHIPS OF MARY RUSSELL

MITFORD: As Recorded in Letters from her Literary Correspondents. Edited by the Rev. A. G. L'Estrange, Editor of "The Life of Mary Russell Mitford," and Author of "The Life of the Rev. W. Harness," &c. 2 vols. crown 8vo. 21s.

Among other persons whose letters are recorded in these volumes are:—Lady Dacre, The Duke of Devonshire, Lord St. Germans, Lord Holland, Sir William Elford, Dean Milman, Rev. A. Dyce, Mrs. Trollope, Mrs. Hofland, Mrs. S. C. Hall, Mrs. Jameson, Mrs. Opie, Mrs. Clive, Mrs. Hemans, Miss Edgeworth, Miss Strickland, Miss Martineau, Miss Barrett, Miss de Quincey, Miss Jephson, Miss Porden, Miss Sedgwick, Joanna Baillie, William Cobbett, Macready, Kemble, Douglas Jerrold, Walter Savage Landor, Eliot Warburton, Barry Cornwall, John Ruskin, Tom Taylor, Serjeant Talfourd, Crabbe Robinson, Charles Young, Digby Starkey, Bayard Taylor, George Darley, George Ticknor, N. P. Willis, the Howitts, &c.

"Few collections of miscellaneous letters are so well worth reading as these. The ideas of the writers are so various and the styles so different, that it is impossible to grow weary of them. Entirely apart from their connection with Miss Mitford, there is much to please and much to be learnt from the book. Everyone will find some favourite author or poet among the correspondents, and therefore find it worth their while to read at least some of the letters included in the present volumes. Mr. L'Estrange has performed his task with care, and it has evidently been a labour of love."—*Morning Post.*

"To have been a friend of Mary Russell Mitford is, paraphrasing the language of Steele, a liberal education. As a correspondent, Miss Mitford was hardly inferior to Cowper, her faculty being derived from her mother, whose letters are admirable specimens of easy, confidential, sympathetic communication. These letters are all written as to one whom the writers love and revere. Miss Barrett is one of Miss Mitford's correspondents, all of whom seem to be inspired with a sense of excellence in the mind they are invoking. Their letters are extremely interesting, and they strike out recollections, opinions, criticisms, which will hold the reader's delighted and serious attention."—*Daily Telegraph.*

"In this singular and probably unique book Miss Mitford is painted, not in letters of her own nor in letters written of her, but in letters addressed to her; and a true idea is thus conveyed of her talent, her disposition, and of the impression she made upon her friends. It seldom happens that anyone, however distinguished, receives such a number of letters well worth reading as were addressed to Miss Mitford; and the letters from her correspondents are not only from interesting persons, but are in themselves interesting."—*St. James's Gazette.*

"One of the first successes of the literary season has been made by 'Miss Mitford's Friendships.' It is a thoroughly literary book, in which literary subjects are dealt with by writers who were called upon by their profession to handle them. It possesses a singular interest from the effective manner in which it transports the reader into the past."—*Standard.*

"No one has left a happier memory behind her than Miss Mitford. Her books are fresh with all the freshness of country life. The letters addressed to her are extremely miscellaneous; there are some characteristic ones from Cobbett, some really clever ones from Sir William Elford, and some full of pleasant gossip from Mrs. Trollope."—*Athenæum.*

"Twelve years have passed since 'The Life of Mary Russell Mitford' was published, and it might fairly be thought that the public was quite ready and willing to hear more of one of the most popular women and vivacious writers of the generation preceding our own. The two collections, therefore, fit and complete each other."—*Pall Mall Gazette.*

"Some of the most delightful specimens of friendly and literary correspondence which exist in the English language. On the various interesting reminiscences of Miss Mitford's contemporaries we cannot here enlarge, but they will repay the reader's search."—*The Queen.*

"Mr. L'Estrange gives his readers several letters written by Miss Mitford, and these will be found even more interesting than the others."—*Globe.*

"This book is in many parts highly attractive. Not the least pleasant passages in the collection are casual notices of passing acquaintances and strangers."—*Saturday Review.*

1

MESSRS. HURST AND BLACKETT'S

NEW WORKS—*Continued.*

COURT LIFE BELOW STAIRS; or, LONDON UNDER THE FIRST GEORGES, 1714—1760. By J. FITZGERALD MOLLOY. *Second Edition.* 2 vols. crown 8vo. 21s.

"If the two volumes which Mr. Molloy has given to the world have no great claim to originality, it may at least be said of them that they recall scenes and anecdotes which will long continue to amuse those who read only for amusement. Mr. Molloy has a certain power of description which to the taste of many readers will be more telling than either style or wit. We may mention as a specimen the description of the Drawing-Room at St. James's, which is written in a very graphic and vivacious manner, and contains many good stories about lords and ladies which are neatly and effectively put together."—*St James's Gazette.*

"In these volumes there is a good deal of that kind of information which is valued by readers of society journals. Mr. Molloy produces some curious anecdotes which have not before appeared in print, and he is always lively."—*Pall Mall.*

WITH THE CONNAUGHT RANGERS IN QUARTERS, CAMP, AND ON LEAVE. By GENERAL E. H. MAXWELL, C.B, Author of "Griffin, Ahoy!" 1 vol. demy 8vo. With Illustrations. 15s.

ROYAL WINDSOR. By W. HEPWORTH DIXON. *Second Edition.* Volumes I. and II. Demy 8vo. 30s.

"'Royal Windsor' follows in the same lines as 'Her Majesty's Tower,' and aims at weaving a series of popular sketches of striking events which centre round Windsor Castle. Mr. Dixon makes everything vivid and picturesque. Those who liked 'Her Majesty's Tower' will find these volumes equally pleasant."—*Athenæum.*

"A truly fine and interesting book. It is a valuable contribution to English history; worthy of Mr. Dixon's fame, worthy of its grand subject."—*Morning Post.*

"Mr. Dixon has supplied us with a highly entertaining book. 'Royal Windsor' is eminently a popular work, bristling with anecdotes and amusing sketches of historical characters."—*Examiner.*

"These volumes will find favour with the widest circle of readers. From the first days of Norman Windsor to the Plantagenet period Mr. Dixon tells the story of this famous castle in his own picturesque, bright, and vigorous way."—*Daily Telegraph.*

"Mr. Hepworth Dixon has found a congenial subject in 'Royal Windsor.' Under the sanction of the Queen, he has enjoyed exceptional opportunities of most searching and complete investigation of the Royal House and every other part of Windsor Castle, in and out, above ground and below ground."—*Daily News.*

VOLS. III. AND IV. OF ROYAL WINDSOR. By W. HEPWORTH DIXON. *Second Edition.* Demy 8vo. 30s. Completing the Work.

"Readers of all classes will feel a genuine regret to think that these volumes contain the last of Mr. Dixon's vivid and lively sketches of English history. His hand retained its cunning to the last, and these volumes show an increase in force and dignity."—*Athenæum.*

"Mr. Dixon's is the picturesque way of writing history Scene after scene is brought before us in the most effective way. His book is not only pleasant reading, but full of information."—*Graphic.*

GRIFFIN, AHOY! A Yacht Cruise to the LEVANT, and Wanderings in EGYPT, SYRIA, THE HOLY LAND, GREECE, and ITALY in 1881. By GENERAL E. H. MAXWELL, C.B. One vol. demy 8vo. With Illustrations. 15s.

"The cruise of the *Griffin* affords bright and amusing reading from its beginning to its end. General Maxwell writes in a frank and easy style—*Morning Post.*

"General Maxwell writes with a facile and seductive pen, and in his chapter on the Lebanon and anti-Lebanon he touches on comparatively unknown regions, where it is instructive as well as pleasurable to follow him."—*Daily Telegraph.*

MESSRS. HURST AND BLACKETT'S
NEW WORKS—*Continued.*

HISTORY OF TWO QUEENS: CATHARINE
OF ARAGON and ANNE BOLEYN. By W. Hepworth Dixon.
Second Edition. Vols. 1 & 2. Demy 8vo. 30s.

"In two handsome volumes Mr. Dixon here gives us the first instalment of a new historical work on a most attractive subject. The book is in many respects a favourable specimen of Mr. Dixon's powers. It is the most painstaking and elaborate that he has yet written. . . . . On the whole, we may say that the book is one which will sustain the reputation of its author as a writer of great power and versatility, that it gives a new aspect to many an old subject, and presents in a very striking light some of the most recent discoveries in English history."—*Athenæum.*

"In these volumes the author exhibits in a signal manner his special powers and finest endowments. It is obvious that the historian has been at especial pains to justify his reputation, to strengthen his hold upon the learned, and also to extend his sway over the many who prize an attractive style and interesting narrative more highly than laborious research and philosophic insight."—*Morning Post.*

"The thanks of all students of English history are due to Mr. Hepworth Dixon for his clever and original work, 'History of two Queens.' The book is a valuable contribution to English history."—*Daily News*

VOLS. III. & IV. OF THE HISTORY OF TWO
QUEENS: CATHARINE OF ARAGON and ANNE BOLEYN. By W. Hepworth Dixon. *Second Edition.* Demy 8vo. Price 30s. Completing the Work.

"These concluding volumes of Mr. Dixon's 'History of two Queens' will be perused with keen interest by thousands of readers. Whilst no less valuable to the student, they will be far more enthralling to the general reader than the earlier half of the history. Every page of what may be termed Anne Boleyn's story affords a happy illustration of the author's vivid and picturesque style. The work should be found in every library."—*Post.*

HISTORY OF WILLIAM PENN, Founder of
Pennsylvania. By W. Hepworth Dixon. A New Library Edition 1 vol. demy 8vo. With Portrait. 12s.

"Mr. Dixon's 'William Penn' is, perhaps, the best of his books. He has now revised and issued it with the addition of much fresh matter. It is now offered in a sumptuous volume, matching with Mr. Dixon's recent books, to a new generation of readers, who will thank Mr. Dixon for his interesting and instructive memoir of one of the worthies of England."—*Examiner.*

VOLS. III. & IV. OF HER MAJESTY'S TOWER.
By W. HEPWORTH DIXON. DEDICATED BY EXPRESS PERMISSION TO THE QUEEN. Completing the Work. *Third Edition.* Demy 8vo. 30s.

FREE RUSSIA. By W. Hepworth Dixon. *Third*
Edition. 2 vols. 8vo. With Coloured Illustrations. 30s.

"Mr. Dixon's book will be certain not only to interest but to please its readers and it deserves to do so. It contains a great deal that is worthy of attention, and is likely to produce a very useful effect."—*Saturday Review.*

THE SWITZERS. By W. Hepworth Dixon.
Third Edition. 1 vol. demy 8vo. 15s.

"A lively, interesting, and altogether novel book on Switzerland. It is full of valuable information on social, political, and ecclesiastical questions, and, like all Mr. Dixon's books, is eminently readable."—*Daily News.*

4

MESSRS. HURST AND BLACKETT'S
NEW WORKS—*Continued.*

MONSIEUR GUIZOT IN PRIVATE LIFE (1787-1874). By His Daughter, Madame DE WITT. Translated by Mrs. SIMPSON. 1 vol. demy 8vo. 15s.

"Madame de Witt has done justice to her father's memory in an admirable record of his life. Mrs. Simpson's translation of this singularly interesting book is in accuracy and grace worthy of the original and of the subject."—*Saturday Review.*

"This book was well worth translating. Mrs. Simpson has written excellent English, while preserving the spirit of the French."—*The Times.*

"We cannot but feel grateful for the picture that Mme. de Witt has given us of her father in his home. It is a work for which no one can be better qualified than a daughter who thoroughly understood and sympathised with him."—*Guardian.*

"M. Guizot stands out in the pages of his daughter's excellent biography a distinct and life-like figure. He is made to speak to us in his own person. The best part of the book consists of a number of his letters, in which he freely unfolds his feelings and opinions, and draws with unconscious boldness the outlines of his forcible and striking character."—*Pall Mall Gazette.*

WORDS OF HOPE AND COMFORT TO THOSE IN SORROW. Dedicated by Permission to THE QUEEN. *Fourth Edition.* 1 vol. small 4to. 5s. bound.

"These letters, the work of a pure and devout spirit, deserve to find many readers. They are greatly superior to the average of what is called religious literature."—*Athenæum.*

"The writer of the tenderly-conceived letters in this volume was Mrs. Julius Hare, a sister of Mr. Maurice. They are instinct with the devout submissiveness and fine sympathy which we associate with the name of Maurice; but in her there is added a winningness of tact, and sometimes, too, a directness of language, which we hardly find even in the brother. The letters were privately printed and circulated, and were found to be the source of much comfort, which they cannot fail to afford now to a wide circle. A sweetly-conceived memorial poem, bearing the well-known initials, 'E. H. P.', gives a very faithful outline of the life."—*British Quarterly Review.*

"This touching and most comforting work is dedicated to THE QUEEN, who took a gracious interest in its first appearance, when printed for private circulation, and found comfort in its pages, and has now commanded its publication, that the world in general may profit by it. A more practical and heart-stirring appeal to the afflicted we have never examined."—*Standard.*

"These letters are exceptionally graceful and touching, and may be read with profit."—*Graphic.*

LIFE OF MOSCHELES; WITH SELECTIONS FROM HIS DIARIES AND CORRESPONDENCE. By His WIFE. 2 vols. large post 8vo. With Portrait. 24s.

"This life of Moscheles will be a valuable book of reference for the musical historian, for the contents extend over a period of threescore years, commencing with 1794, and ending at 1870. We need scarcely state that all the portions of Moscheles' diary which refer to his intercourse with Beethoven, Hummel, Weber, Czerny, Spontini, Rossini, Auber, Halévy, Schumann, Cherubini, Spohr, Mendelssohn, F. David, Chopin, J B. Cramer, Clementi, John Field, Habeneck, Hauptmann, Kalkbrenner, Kiesewetter, O. Klingemann, Lablache, Dragonetti, Sontag, Persiani, Malibran, Paganini, Rachel, Ronzi de Begnis, De Beriot, Ernst, Donzelli, Cinti-Damoreau, Chelard, Bochsa, Laporte, Charles Kemble, Schröder-Devrient, Mrs. Siddons, Sir H. Bishop, Sir G. Smart, Staudigl, Thalberg, Berlioz, Velluti, C. Young, Balfe, Braham, and many other artists of note in their time, will recall a flood of recollections. Moscheles writes fairly of what is called the 'Music of the Future,' and his judgments on Herr Wagner, Dr. Liszt, Rubenstein, Dr. von Bülow, Litolff, &c., whether as composers or executants, are in a liberal spirit. He recognizes cheerfully the talents of our native artists: Sir S. Bennett, Mr. Macfarren, Madame Goddard, Mr. J. Barnett, Mr. Hullah, Mr. A. Sullivan, &c. The volumes are full of amusing anecdotes."—*Athenæum.*

MESSRS. HURST AND BLACKETT'S
NEW WORKS—*Continued.*

A YOUNG SQUIRE OF THE SEVENTEENTH
CENTURY, from the Papers of CHRISTOPHER JEAFFRESON, of Dullingham House, Cambridgeshire. Edited by JOHN CORDY JEAFFRESON, Author of "A Book about Doctors," &c. 2 vols. crown 8vo. 21s.

"Two volumes of very attractive matter:—letters which illustrate agriculture, commerce, war, love, and social manners, accounts of passing public events, and details which are not to be found in the Gazettes, and which come with singular freshness from private letters."—*Athenæum.*

"Two agreeable and important volumes. They deserve to be placed on library shelves with Pepys, Evelyn, and Reresby. The Jeaffreson letters add very much to our knowledge of other people, and of other acts than those recorded by Pepys, Evelyn, and Reresby, and are pleasantly supplementary in sketches of contemporaneous men and manners."—*Notes and Queries.*

MY YOUTH, BY SEA AND LAND, FROM 1809 TO
1816. By CHARLES LOFTUS, formerly of the Royal Navy, late of the Coldstream Guards. 2 vols. crown 8vo. 21s.

"Major Loftus played the part allotted to him with honour and ability, and he relates the story of his life with spirit and vigour. Some of his sea stories are as laughable as anything in ' Peter Simple,' while his adventures on shore remind us of Charles Lever in his freshest days. A more genial, pleasant, wholesome book we have not often read."—*Standard.*

MY LIFE, FROM 1815 TO 1849. By CHARLES LOFTUS,
Author of "My Youth by Sea and Land." 2 vols. crown 8vo. 21s.

"The praise which the *Athenæum* gave to the first portion of Major Loftus's work, may be fairly awarded to the second. These reminiscences are pleasantly told. There is a cheeriness about them which communicates itself to the reader."—*Athenæum.*

"A thoroughly interesting and readable book, which we heartily recommend . s one of the most characteristic autobiographies we ever read."—*Standard.*

A LEGACY: Being the Life and Remains of JOHN
MARTIN, Schoolmaster and Poet. Written and Edited by the Author of "JOHN HALIFAX." 2 vols. crown 8vo. With Portrait. 21s.

"A remarkable book. It records the life, work, aspirations, and death of a schoolmaster and poet, of lowly birth but ambitious soul. His writings brim with vivid thought, touches of poetic sentiment, and trenchant criticism of men and books, expressed in scholarly language."—*Guardian.*

THE VILLAGE OF PALACES; or, Chronicles of
Chelsea. By the Rev. A. G. L'ESTRANGE. 2 vols. crown 8vo. 21s.

"Mr. L'Estrange has much to tell of the various public institutions associated with Chelsea. Altogether his volumes show some out-of-the-way research, and are written in a lively and gossipping style."—*The Times.*

"Mr. L'Estrange tells us much that is interesting about Chelsea. We take leave of this most charming book with a hearty recommendation of it to our readers."—*Spectator.*

COSITAS ESPANOLAS; OR, EVERY-DAY LIFE IN
SPAIN. By Mrs. HARVEY, of Ickwell-Bury. *2nd Edition.* 8vo. 15s.

"A charming book; fresh, lively, and amusing."—*Morning Post.*

MEMOIRS OF QUEEN HORTENSE, MOTHER
OF NAPOLEON III. Cheaper Edition, in 1 vol. 6s.

"A biography of the beautiful and unhappy Queen, more satisfactory than any we have yet met with."—*Daily News.*

WORKS BY VARIOUS AUTHORS.

WORKS BY THE AUTHOR OF 'JOHN HALIFAX.'

Each in One Volume, elegantly printed, bound, and illustrated, price 5s.

JOHN HALIFAX, GENTLEMAN.	CHRISTIAN'S MISTAKE.
A WOMAN'S THOUGHTS ABOUT WOMEN.	A NOBLE LIFE.
	HANNAH.
A LIFE FOR A LIFE.	THE UNKIND WORD.
NOTHING NEW.	A BRAVE LADY.
MISTRESS AND MAID.	STUDIES FROM LIFE.
THE WOMAN'S KINGDOM.	YOUNG MRS. JARDINE.

WORKS BY THE AUTHOR OF 'SAM SLICK.'

Each in One Volume, elegantly printed, bound, and illustrated, price 5s.

NATURE AND HUMAN NATURE.	THE OLD JUDGE ; OR, LIFE IN A COLONY.
WISE SAWS AND MODERN INSTANCES.	TRAITS OF AMERICAN HUMOUR.

THE AMERICANS AT HOME.

WORKS BY MRS. OLIPHANT.

Each in One Volume, elegantly printed, bound, and illustrated, price 5s.

ADAM GRAEME.	THE LIFE OF THE REV. EDWARD IRVING.
THE LAIRD OF NORLAW.	
AGNES.	A ROSE IN JUNE.

PHŒBE, JUNIOR.

WORKS BY GEORGE MAC DONALD, LL.D.

Each in One Volume, elegantly printed, bound, and illustrated, price 5s.

DAVID ELGINBROD.	ALEC FORBES.
ROBERT FALCONER.	SIR GIBBIE.

HURST & BLACKETT'S STANDARD LIBRARY
OF CHEAP EDITIONS OF
POPULAR MODERN WORKS,

ILLUSTRATED BY SIR J. GILBERT, MILLAIS, HUNT, LEECH, FOSTER, POYNTER, TENNIEL, SANDYS, HUGHES, SAMBOURNE, &c.

Each in a Single Volume, elegantly printed, bound, and illustrated, price 5s.

---

1. SAM SLICK'S NATURE AND HUMAN NATURE.

"The first volume of Messrs. Hurst and Blackett's Standard Library of Cheap Editions forms a very good beginning to what will doubtless be a very successful undertaking. 'Nature and Human Nature' is one of the best of Sam Slick's witty and humorous productions, and is well entitled to the large circulation which it cannot fail to obtain in its present convenient and cheap shape. The volume combines with the great recommendations of a clear, bold type, and good paper, the lesser but attractive merits of being well illustrated and elegantly bound."—*Post.*

2. JOHN HALIFAX, GENTLEMAN.

"This is a very good and a very interesting work. It is designed to trace the career from boyhood to age of a perfect man—a Christian gentleman; and it abounds in incident both well and highly wrought. Throughout it is conceived in a high spirit, and written with great ability. This cheap and handsome new edition is worthy to pass freely from hand to hand as a gift book in many households."—*Examiner.*

3. THE CRESCENT AND THE CROSS.
BY ELIOT WARBURTON.

"Independent of its value as an original narrative, and its useful and interesting information, this work is remarkable for the colouring power and play of fancy with which its descriptions are enlivened. Among its greatest and most lasting charms is its reverent and serious spirit."—*Quarterly Review.*

4. NATHALIE. By JULIA KAVANAGH.

"'Nathalie' is Miss Kavanagh's best imaginative effort. Its manner is gracious and attractive. Its matter is good."—*Athenæum.*

5. A WOMAN'S THOUGHTS ABOUT WOMEN.
BY THE AUTHOR OF "JOHN HALIFAX, GENTLEMAN."

"A book of sound counsel. It is one of the most sensible works of its kind, well-written, true-hearted, and altogether practical. Whoever wishes to give advice to a young lady may thank the author for means of doing so."—*Examiner.*

6. ADAM GRAEME. By MRS. OLIPHANT.

"A story awakening genuine emotions of interest and delight by its admirable pictures of Scottish life and scenery. The author sets before us the essential attributes of Christian virtue, with a delicacy, power, and truth which can hardly be surpassed."—*Post.*

7. SAM SLICK'S WISE SAWS & MODERN INSTANCES.

"The reputation of this book will stand as long as that of Scott's or Bulwer's Novels. Its remarkable originality and happy descriptions of American life still continue the subject of universal admiration."—*Messenger.*

8. CARDINAL WISEMAN'S RECOLLECTIONS OF THE LAST FOUR POPES.

"A picturesque book on Rome and its ecclesiastical sovereigns, by an eloquent Roman Catholic. Cardinal Wiseman has treated a special subject with so much geniality, that his recollections will excite no ill-feeling in those who are most conscientiously opposed to every idea of human infallibility represented in Papal domination."—*Athenæum.*

9. A LIFE FOR A LIFE.
BY THE AUTHOR OF "JOHN HALIFAX, GENTLEMAN."

"In 'A Life for a Life' the author is fortunate in a good subject, and has produced a work of strong effect."—*Athenæum.*

10. THE OLD COURT SUBURB. By LEIGH HUNT.

"A delightful book, that will be welcome to all readers, and most welcome to those who have a love for the best kinds of reading."—*Examiner.*

HURST & BLACKETT'S STANDARD LIBRARY

11. MARGARET AND HER BRIDESMAIDS.

"We recommend all who are in search of a fascinating novel to read this work for themselves. They will find it well worth their while. There are a freshness and originality about it quite charming."—*Athenæum.*

12. THE OLD JUDGE. By SAM SLICK.

"The publications included in this Library have all been of good quality; many give information while they entertain, and of that class the book before us is a specimen. The manner in which the Cheap Editions forming the series is produced, deserves especial mention. The paper and print are unexceptionable; there is a steel engraving in each volume, and the outsides of them will satisfy the purchaser who likes to see books in handsome uniform."—*Examiner.*

13. DARIEN. By ELIOT WARBURTON.

"This last production of the author of 'The Crescent and the Cross' has the same elements of a very wide popularity. It will please its thousands."—*Globe.*

14. FAMILY ROMANCE.

BY SIR BERNARD BURKE, ULSTER KING OF ARMS.

"It were impossible to praise too highly this most interesting book."—*Standard.*

15. THE LAIRD OF NORLAW. By MRS. OLIPHANT

"The 'Laird of Norlaw' fully sustains the author's high reputation."—*Sunday Times*

16. THE ENGLISHWOMAN IN ITALY.

"Mrs. Gretton's book is interesting, and full of opportune instruction."—*Times*

17. NOTHING NEW.

BY THE AUTHOR OF "JOHN HALIFAX, GENTLEMAN."

"'Nothing New' displays all those superior merits which have made 'John Halifax' one of the most popular works of the day."—*Post.*

18. FREER'S LIFE OF JEANNE D'ALBRET.

"Nothing can be more interesting than Miss Freer's story of the life of Jeanne D'Albret, and the narrative is as trustworthy as it is attractive."—*Post.*

19. THE VALLEY OF A HUNDRED FIRES.

BY THE AUTHOR OF "MARGARET AND HER BRIDESMAIDS."

"If asked to classify this work, we should give it a place between 'John Halifax' and 'The Caxtons.'"—*Standard.*

20. THE ROMANCE OF THE FORUM.

BY PETER BURKE, SERGEANT AT LAW.

"A work of singular interest, which can never fail to charm."—*Illustrated News.*

21. ADELE. By JULIA KAVANAGH.

"'Adele' is the best work we have read by Miss Kavanagh; it is a charming story, full of delicate character-painting."—*Athenæum.*

22. STUDIES FROM LIFE.

BY THE AUTHOR OF "JOHN HALIFAX, GENTLEMAN."

"These 'Studies from Life' are remarkable for graphic power and observation. The book will not diminish the reputation of the accomplished author."—*Saturday Review.*

23. GRANDMOTHER'S MONEY.

"We commend 'Grandmother's Money' to readers in search of a good novel. The characters are true to human nature, and the story is interesting."—*Athenæum.*

24. A BOOK ABOUT DOCTORS. By J. C. JEAFFRESON.

"A delightful book."—*Athenæum.* "A book to be read and re-read; fit for the study as well as the drawing-room table and the circulating library."—*Lancet.*

HURST & BLACKETT'S STANDARD LIBRARY

25. NO CHURCH.

"We advise all who have the opportunity to read this book."—*Athenæum.*

26. MISTRESS AND MAID.

BY THE AUTHOR OF "JOHN HALIFAX, GENTLEMAN."

"A good wholesome book, gracefully written, and as pleasant to read as it is instructive."—*Athenæum.* "A charming tale charmingly told."—*Standard.*

27. LOST AND SAVED. By HON. MRS. NORTON.

"'Lost and Saved' will be read with eager interest. It is a vigorous novel."—*Times.*
"A novel of rare excellence. It is Mrs. Norton's best prose work."—*Examiner.*

28. LES MISERABLES. By VICTOR HUGO.

AUTHORISED COPYRIGHT ENGLISH TRANSLATION.

"The merits of 'Les Miserables' do not merely consist in the conception of it as a whole; it abounds with details of unequalled beauty. M. Victor Hugo has stamped upon every page the hall-mark of genius."—*Quarterly Review.*

29. BARBARA'S HISTORY. By AMELIA B. EDWARDS.

"It is not often that we light upon a novel of so much merit and interest as 'Barbara's History.' It is a work conspicuous for taste and literary culture. It is a very graceful and charming book, with a well-managed story, clearly-cut characters, and sentiments expressed with an exquisite elocution. It is a book which the world will like."—*Times.*

30. LIFE OF THE REV. EDWARD IRVING.

BY MRS. OLIPHANT.

"A good book on a most interesting theme."—*Times.*
"A truly interesting and most affecting memoir. Irving's Life ought to have a niche in every gallery of religious biography."—*Saturday Review.*

31. ST. OLAVE'S.

"This charming novel is the work of one who possesses a great talent for writing, as well as experience and knowledge of the world.'—*Athenæum.*

32. SAM SLICK'S AMERICAN HUMOUR.

"Dip where you will into this lottery of fun, you are sure to draw out a prize."—*Post.*

33. CHRISTIAN'S MISTAKE.

BY THE AUTHOR OF "JOHN HALIFAX, GENTLEMAN."

"A more charming story has rarely been written. Even if tried by the standard of the Archbishop of York, we should expect that even he would pronounce 'Christian's Mistake' a novel without a fault."—*Times.*

34. ALEC FORBES. By GEORGE MAC DONALD, LL.D.

"No account of this story would give any idea of the profound interest that pervades the work from the first page to the last."—*Athenæum.*

35. AGNES. By MRS. OLIPHANT.

"'Agnes' is a novel superior to any of Mrs. Oliphant's former works."—*Athenæum.*
"A story whose pathetic beauty will appeal irresistibly to all readers."—*Post.*

36. A NOBLE LIFE.

BY THE AUTHOR OF "JOHN HALIFAX, GENTLEMAN."

"This is one of those pleasant tales in which the author of 'John Halifax' speaks out of a generous heart the purest truths of life."—*Examiner.*

37. NEW AMERICA. By HEPWORTH DIXON.

"A very interesting book. Mr. Dixon has written thoughtfully and well."—*Times.*
"We recommend every one who feels any interest in human nature to read Mr. Dixon's very interesting book."—*Saturday Review.*

38. ROBERT FALCONER. By GEORGE MAC DONALD.

"'Robert Falconer' is a work brimful of life and humour and of the deepest human interest. It is a book to be returned to again and again for the deep and searching knowledge it evinces of human thoughts and feelings."—*Athenæum.*

HURST & BLACKETT'S STANDARD LIBRARY

39. THE WOMAN'S KINGDOM.

BY THE AUTHOR OF "JOHN HALIFAX, GENTLEMAN."

"'The Woman's Kingdom' sustains the author's reputation as a writer of the purest and noblest kind of domestic stories.—*Athenæum.*

40. ANNALS OF AN EVENTFUL LIFE.

BY GEORGE WEBBE DASENT, D.C.L.

"A racy, well-written, and original novel. The interest never flags. The whole work sparkles with wit and humour."—*Quarterly Review.*

41. DAVID ELGINBROD. By GEORGE MAC DONALD.

"The work of a man of genius. It will attract the highest class of readers."—*Times.*

42. A BRAVE LADY. By the Author of "John Halifax."

"A very good novel; a thoughtful, well-written book, showing a tender sympathy with human nature, and permeated by a pure and noble spirit."—*Examiner.*

43. HANNAH. By the Author of "John Halifax."

"A very pleasant, healthy story, well and artistically told. The book is sure of a wide circle of readers. The character of Hannah is one of rare beauty."—*Standard.*

44. SAM SLICK'S AMERICANS AT HOME.

"This is one of the most amusing books that we ever read."—*Standard.*

45. THE UNKIND WORD.

BY THE AUTHOR OF "JOHN HALIFAX, GENTLEMAN."

"The author of 'John Halifax' has written many fascinating stories, but we can call to mind nothing from her pen that has a more enduring charm than the graceful sketches in this work."—*United Service Magazine.*

46. A ROSE IN JUNE. By MRS. OLIPHANT.

"'A Rose in June' is as pretty as its title. The story is one of the best and most touching which we owe to the industry and talent of Mrs. Oliphant, and may hold its own with even 'The Chronicles of Carlingford.'"—*Times.*

47. MY LITTLE LADY. By E. F. POYNTER.

"There is a great deal of fascination about this book. The author writes in a clear, unaffected style; she has a decided gift for depicting character, while the descriptions of scenery convey a distinct pictorial impression to the reader."—*Times.*

48. PHŒBE, JUNIOR. By MRS. OLIPHANT.

"This novel shows great knowledge of human nature. The interest goes on growing to the end. Phœbe is excellently drawn."—*Times.*

49. LIFE OF MARIE ANTOINETTE.

BY PROFESSOR CHARLES DUKE YONGE.

"A work of remarkable merit and interest, which will, we doubt not, become the most popular English history of Marie Antoinette."—*Spectator.*

"This book is well written, and of thrilling interest."—*Academy,*

50. SIR GIBBIE. By GEORGE MAC DONALD, LL.D.

"'Sir Gibbie' is a book of genius."—*Pall Mall Gazette.*

"This book has power, pathos, and humour. There is not a character which is not lifelike."—*Athenæum.*

51. YOUNG MRS. JARDINE.

BY THE AUTHOR OF "JOHN HALIFAX, GENTLEMAN."

"'Young Mrs. Jardine' is a pretty story, written in pure English."—*The Times.*

"There is much good feeling in this book. It is pleasant and wholesome."—*Athenæum.*

52. LORD BRACKENBURY. By AMELIA B. EDWARDS.

"A very readable story. The author has well conceived the purpose of high-class novel-writing, and succeeded in no small measure in attaining it. There is plenty of variety, cheerful dialogue, and general 'verve' in the book."—*Athenæum.*

"'Lord Brackenbury' is pleasant reading from beginning to end."—*Academy.*

THE NEW AND POPULAR NOVELS.
PUBLISHED BY HURST & BLACKETT.

I HAVE LIVED AND LOVED. By Mrs. FOR-
RESTER, Author of " Viva," " Mignon," " My Lord and my Lady,"
&c. 3 vols.

EXCHANGE NO ROBBERY. By M. BETHAM-
EDWARDS, Author of "Kitty," " Doctor Jacob," &c. 2 vols.

A GOLDEN BAR. By the Author of " Christina
North," " Under the Limes," &c. 3 vols.

RED RYVINGTON. By WILLIAM WESTALL, Author
of " Larry Lohengrin," &c. 3 vols.

"Mr. Westall writes of the manufacturing districts with knowledge, and in his
hands the rough Lancashire folk and the grimy purlieus of the cotton towns lend
themselves not unpicturesquely to the needs of fiction."—*Athenæum.*

"One of the most readable novels of the year. The author's interests are wide
and intelligently directed, and his way of describing incident is exceedingly
graphic. The conversations are both interesting and amusing, preserving, as they
do, the racy and humorous manners and modes of expression of the self-made
men who hold them."—*Daily News.*

"A very pleasant and readable tale of English life and manners. The character of Dora, the honest, straightforward English girl, is very charming. Mr. Westall's large circle of readers will welcome this latest effusion from his pen."—*Life.*

GABRIELLE DE BOURDAINE. By Mrs. JOHN
KENT SPENDER, Author of " Godwyn's Ordeal," " Both in the
Wrong," &c. 3 vols.

"We advise all who can enjoy a pretty story, well told, to read 'Gabrielle de
Bourdaine.' It is the best of Mrs. Spender's novels. It is in her character-drawing that the author shows so marked an improvement."—*Standard.*

"'Gabrielle de Bourdaine' is a pleasant story in its quiet and simple way. It is
readable and attractive."—*Athenæum.*

"Like every work of Mrs. Spender's, this novel bears many traces of cultivated
power and deep thought."—*John Bull.*

"This novel is deeply interesting . . . . There are many passages which would
make the reputation of a novelist. Gabrielle is drawn with a powerful pen, and
is a delightful study."—*Scotsman.*

SAINT AND SIBYL. By C. L. PIRKIS, Author of
" A Very Opal," " Wanted, An Heir," &c. 3 vols.

"In 'Saint and Sibyl' there are some excellent pieces of writing, some touches
of poetical art. some highly dramatic scenes, some pretty and pathetic pictures."
—*St. James's Gazette.*

"This story abounds in incident and diversity of character. There are many
striking passages."—*The Queen.*

"A cleverly written, readable story. The two girls, Rose and Sibyl, are ably
contrasted: Sibyl in especial is an original, clever conception."—*Daily News.*

DAISY BERESFORD. By CATHARINE CHILDAR,
Author of " The Future Marquis." 3 vols.

"An admirable novel, which will not fail to extend its author's popularity very
widely."—*John Bull.*

"Several of the characters in 'Daisy Beresford' are cleverly drawn. Two old
maiden aunts are very well done, and the heroine is also good."—*Athenæum.*

"Miss Childar has written a pretty, pleasant story, full of varied character and
entertaining talk. Daisy Beresford is a charming creation."—*Daily News.*

DONOVAN. By EDNA LYALL, Author of " Won by
Waiting." 3 vols.

"'Donovan' is distinctly a novel with a high aim, successfully attained. The
character-drawing is vigorous and truthful."—*Pall Mall Gazette.*

THE NEW AND POPULAR NOVELS.
PUBLISHED BY HURST & BLACKETT.

THE BRANDRETHS. By the Right Hon. A. J. B. Beresford Hope, M.P., Author of "Strictly Tied Up." *Second Edition.* 3 vols.

"In 'The Brandreths' we have a sequel to Mr. Beresford Hope's clever novel of 'Strictly Tied Up,' and we may add that it is a decided improvement on his maiden effort. He has not only laid a firmer grasp on some of those characters which in his earlier work were rather wanting in outline and individuality, but he has secured the interest of his readers by simplifying his story. 'The Brandreths,' although it abounds in the study of personal character, investigating the innermost life and analysing the feelings of the hero, is, nevertheless, in great measure a political novel. Mr. Hope writes of political life and the vicissitudes of parties with the knowledge and experience of a veteran politician. Not a few of the casual pictures of society are exceedingly faithful and lively. We repeat, in conclusion, that the novel is one which will repay careful reading."—*Times.*

"There are many sayings in these volumes—many wise. many witty, many tender, many noble sayings—that we should wish to cite to our readers, but doubtless their pleasure will be greater in finding them out for themselves. The book is full of clever epigrams."—*Standard.*

NEW BABYLON. By Paul Meritt and W. Howell Poole. 3 vols.

"This story is clever and amusing. Vivid and graphic scenes follow in changeful succession."—*Daily Telegraph.*

"'New Babylon' will attract attention at the libraries, where an exciting story is always welcome. The tale hurries along from one stirring incident to another, and compels the reader to admire the inventive power of the writers, and their ingenuity in weaving a complicated series of incidents."—*Era.*

FORTUNE'S MARRIAGE. By Georgiana M. Craik, Author of "Dorcas," "Anne Warwick," &c. 3 vols.

"'Fortune's Marriage' is gentle, tender, and unexaggerated. It is carefully written and has been carefully thought out."—*Daily News.*

"'Fortune's Marriage' is naturally and pleasantly written, like all Miss Craik's stories. Both Fortune and Ronald are thoroughly well drawn."—*St. James's Gazette.*

REDEEMED. By Shirley Smith, Author of "His Last Stake," "All for Herself," &c. 3 vols.

"Her Majesty the Queen and Princess Beatrice have perused this story with great interest, and they have been especially pleased with the manner in which the incidents that led to the death of the Prince Imperial have been introduced in the latter part of the novel."—*Nottingham Guardian.*

THE MERCHANT PRINCE. By John Berwick Harwood, Author of "Lady Flavia," &c. 3 vols.

"A clever, stirring novel."—*Daily Telegraph.*

"'The Merchant Prince' is an interesting story of English commercial life, told quietly and easily in Mr. Harwood's well-known manner."—*Daily News.*

A FAITHFUL LOVER. By Mrs. Macquoid, Author of "Patty," "Diane," &c. 3 vols.

"A pretty, graceful, and agreeable novel, in which there is plenty of charming portraiture and abundance of love-making."—*Illustrated London News.*

IRIS. By Mrs. Randolph, Author of "Gentianella," "Wild Hyacinth," &c. 3 vols.

"'Iris' has all the pleasant characteristics which are peculiar to the writer. As usual, the story is refined, agreeable, and interesting throughout."—*John Bull.*

A BROKEN LILY. By Mrs. Mortimer Collins. 3 vols.

"This novel has many points of interest, and the construction is workmanlike. There is much that is clever and amusing in the story."—*John Bull.*

HURST AND BLACKETT'S
SIX-SHILLING NOVELS

MY LORD AND MY LADY.
By Mrs. Forrester,
Author of "Viva," "Mignon," &c.

" This novel will take a high place among the successes of the season. It is as fresh a novel as it is interesting, as attractive as it is realistically true, as full of novelty of presentment as it is of close study and observation of life."—*World.*

" A love story of considerable interest. The novel is full of surprises, and will serve to while away a leisure hour most agreeably."—*Daily Telegraph.*

" A very capital novel. The great charm about it is that Mrs. Forrester is quite at home in the society which she describes. It is a book to read."—*Standard.*

" Mrs. Forrester's style is so fresh and graphic that the reader is kept under its spell from first to last."—*Post.*

SOPHY:
OR THE ADVENTURES OF A SAVAGE.
By Violet Fane,
Author of "Denzil Place," &c.

" 'Sophy' is the clever and original work of a clever woman. Its merits are of a strikingly unusual kind. It is charged throughout with the strongest human interest. It is, in a word, a novel that will make its mark."—*World.*

" A clever, amusing, and interesting story, well worth reading."—*Post.*

" This novel is as amusing, piquant, droll, and suggestive as it can be. It overflows with humour, nor are there wanting touches of genuine feeling. To considerable imaginative power, the writer joins keen observation."—*Daily News.*

" 'Sophy' throughout displays accurate knowledge of widely differing forms of character, and remarkable breadth of view. It is one of the few current novels that may not impossibly stand the test of time."—*Graphic.*

STRICTLY TIED UP.
By the Right Hon. A. J. B. Beresford Hope, M.P.

" A clever story. In 'Strictly Tied Up' we have vigorous sketches of life in very different circumstances and conditions. We have the incisive portraiture of character that shows varied knowledge of mankind. We have a novel, besides, which may be read with profit as well as pleasure."—*Times.*

" 'Strictly Tied Up' is entertaining. It is in every sense a novel conceived in a light and happy vein. The scheme of the story is well proportioned and worked out in all its complications with much care and skill."—*Athenæum.*

" This novel may be described as a comedy of life and character. There is humour as well as excitement in the book, and not a few of the descriptions both of people and scenery are exceedingly graphic and piquant."—*Saturday Review.*

HIS LITTLE MOTHER: and Other Tales.
By the Author of "John Halifax, Gentleman."

" This is an interesting book, written in a pleasant manner, and full of shrewd observation and kindly feeling. It is a book that will be read with interest, and that cannot be lightly forgotten."—*St. James's Gazette.*

" The Author of 'John Halifax' always writes with grace and feeling, and never more so than in the present volume."—*Morning Post.*

" 'His Little Mother' is one of those pathetic stories which the author tells better than anybody else."—*John Bull.*

" This book is written with all Mrs. Craik's grace of style, the chief charm of which, after all, is its simplicity."—*Glasgow Herald.*

" We cordially recommend 'His Little Mother.' The story is most affecting. The volume is full of lofty sentiments and noble aspirations, and none can help feeling better after its perusal."—*Court Journal.*

LONDON: HURST AND BLACKETT, PUBLISHERS.